# THIS SIDE OF HEAVEN

Shy and retiring but intelligent and pretty, Sylvie is invited to stay with her dead mother's cousin, Lady Carluke. She becomes very fond of Lady Carluke, but believes that her son, Edward, is a fortune-hunting ladykiller. Edward's current girlfriend, the beautiful, sophisticated Diantha, makes no secret of her jealousy of Edward's pretty cousin. Sylvie, for her part, does not at first understand the feelings that are taking shape in her heart.

JULIET GRAY

# THIS SIDE OF HEAVEN

*Complete and Unabridged*

**LINFORD**
*Leicester*

First published in Great Britain

First Linford Edition
published 1997

British Library CIP Data

Gray, Juliet, *1933*–
    This side of heaven.—Large print ed.—
    Linford romance library
    1. Love stories
    2. Large type books
    I. Title
    823.9'14 [F]

    ISBN 0–7089–5114–7

Published by
F. A. Thorpe (Publishing) Ltd.
Anstey, Leicestershire

Set by Words & Graphics Ltd.
Anstey, Leicestershire
Printed and bound in Great Britain by
T. J. Press (Padstow) Ltd., Padstow, Cornwall

This book is printed on acid-free paper

# 1

**D**ESCENDING the wide, sweeping staircase with a book in her hand, Sylvie was brought to a sudden halt by the sound of voices in the hall below her. A man's, deep and drawling, a woman's, light and very confident.

Halfway down the stairs, hidden by shadows, she looked down at the couple, her heart quickening. The man was tall, powerfully built, impressive and very handsome. The white streak in his dark hair told her that he was a Carluke. His companion was a very lovely woman whose fashionable elegance immediately made Sylvie feel that her simple frock was rather dowdy.

Her glance returned to the man.

So that was Edward Carluke. He was very like the portrait that she had studied with so much interest when she had first arrived at the Hall. Strong, rather sensual good looks, dark of hair and eye, a hint of arrogance about him that most women would probably find attractive. And Sylvie knew all about his reputation where women were concerned. He was a light-hearted lover, a womanizer, a rake.

Studying him as he crossed the hall and bent to pull the ears of the spaniel who thumped her tail in lazy greeting without stirring from her place, Sylvie wondered if she was going to like him. It was not necessary to like him, of course. But it would no doubt please his mother who was being very kind to her — and it would be more comfortable if she were to stay for any length of time beneath his roof.

The woman he had brought with him looked about her with an interest that betrayed that it was her first visit to Chase Hall, the home of the Carlukes for generations.

It was Sylvie's first visit, too. But she

had immediately felt at home within its walls. Her mother had spoken so often of the days when she had been a frequent guest at the Hall that Sylvie felt she knew and loved the place without ever expecting to see it. For Chase Hall was a long way from her home in Cornwall. Yet here she was at the warm invitation of Lady Carluke, her dead mother's cousin.

The woman pulled off her close-fitting turban and shook out a mass of shining curls of an auburn such as Sylvie had always admired. She disliked her own pale blonde hair that fell past her shoulders with scarcely a wave or a curl to its name.

"But it's quite baronial, darling." The lovely voice lilted the words. "I'm impressed."

She was so beautiful, so self-assured, that Sylvie immediately felt that her own very ordinary prettiness was cast into shade.

Edward Carluke turned. "I daresay you'll gather some excellent copy for the new book while you are here," he said lightly. He drew her hand through his arm. "My mother will be in her sitting-room at this hour. We're just in time for tea. Come along and be introduced." His smile held a warmth that softened a slight harshness in the sensual face. It was a very attractive smile, Sylvie decided dispassionately. No wonder women liked him so well, responded so readily to the famous Carluke charm.

She decided to slip back to her room, having no desire to meet Edward and his lovely friend before she had changed her dress and brushed her hair and applied a little defensive make-up.

As she turned to re-mount the stairs, the edge of the balustrade caught the corner of the book in her hand. It fell with a clatter and tumbled down several steps before coming to rest.

Edward Carluke turned swiftly, strode to the foot of the stairs. He looked up at the slim figure in the shadows, a frown in his dark eyes. "Who the devil are you?" he demanded.

Sylvie's chin shot up at his tone. She was a little shy, a little unsure of herself, but she did not lack for spirit.

She walked down towards him, pausing to retrieve the book, very conscious that his eyes regarded her with suspicion . . . and that the woman's eyes sparkled with a little malicious amusement. She supposed it must seem that she had been spying on them, she thought, and a faint colour dawned in her face.

"How do you do?" she said as lightly as she could. "You are Edward, of course." She smiled with a hint of shyness, held out her hand. "I'm Sylvie Waring."

He ignored the outstretched hand. "Yes, I'm Edward Carluke." His frown deepened. "Who the devil are you?" he repeated, staring at the slip of a girl in an unfashionable frock, her long, pale hair framing a small and absurdly youthful face.

Sylvie's hand fell to her side. She conceived an instant dislike of a rude and arrogant man. "I'm your second cousin or some such thing," she said coldly. "Your mother asked me to stay."

"Indeed? Cousins, are we? Well, I've never heard of you, I'm afraid." His tone was a trifle curt and unwelcoming. It was not the first time that his mother had tried her hand at match-making and he suspected this to be another of her schemes. But he was astonished that his usually perceptive and very shrewd mother should suppose that he would be at all interested in a gauche young girl. Of course, she could not have known that he would return to the Hall with the beautiful Diantha Craig and be entirely indifferent to the existence of any other woman for the moment.

"Oh? But I've heard so much about you," Sylvie said sweetly, her tone implying that none of it had been flattering.

Diantha moved forward, laying a hand on his arm. "Won't you introduce me to your little cousin, darling?" Her smile, her manner, was cool, amused, rather patronizing.

Sylvie felt about thirteen instead of twenty — just as the woman had obviously intended. Her eyes sparkled with sudden indignation. It was obvious that the woman thought she was a nobody. She might not be elegant or sophisticated or used to moving in fashionable circles but she was the daughter of a very well known and very wealthy man. She did not doubt that his name must be known to Edward Carluke and his snobby friend.

The snobby friend turned out to be Diantha Craig, the successful writer of romantic novels. But Sylvie did not allow the merest flicker of recognition or interest to touch her polite smile or her voice as she acknowledged the introduction.

She turned back to Edward Carluke, held out the book that had betrayed her presence on the stairs. "I wonder if you would give that to your mother with my compliments and tell her that I've taken Hero for a walk."

The spaniel thumped her tail once more at the mention of her name but made no effort to rise in response to another familiar word.

A little smile leaped to Edward's dark eyes. "I don't think that suggestion finds much favour, you know," he drawled. "And it isn't very practical unless you particularly enjoy walking in the rain. I think my mother would prefer you to join us for tea, anyway."

Sylvie understood the dry meaning in the light words. She knew just why she had been invited to Chase Hall. No doubt he knew, too. It was scarcely surprising that he was not prepared to extend a welcome and did not mean to like her. Well, he need not think that she approved or would agree to his mother's scheme for marrying them off. She did not like *him*!

The Carluke fortunes were at very low ebb. They had never recovered from the death duties payable on Edward's succession to the title, apparently. It seemed that marriage to the only child of a very wealthy financier would solve many of his problems. No doubt his mother believed that Sylvie would be pleased to marry a baronet and provide an heir for the estate. She suspected that her father was all in favour of the match, too. Certainly he had urged her to accept the invitation to Chase Hall, reminding her that her poor mother and Lady Carluke had been cousins, pointing out that a quiet and sheltered life in a remote part of Cornwall was no life for a young girl and that it was time she thought about men and marriage.

Curiosity rather than cupidity had brought Sylvie to Cumbria. She had felt a natural interest in the Hall, described so often and with such affection by her mother. She had wished to meet and make friends with members of her family who were strangers. Maude Carluke had once been a famous beauty and a society hostess but now she was a near-invalid with a heart complaint that curtailed her activities. And Sylvie had been very curious to know more of the cousin who was always hitting the headlines because of his women, his fast cars, his wild way of life.

When she was very young, Sylvie had woven foolish dreams about the handsome, wayward Edward Carluke. Now, having met him at last, she was not impressed by him.

She had arrived at the Hall to find that he was away, staying with friends. She had been warmly welcomed by his mother who exclaimed over Sylvie's likeness to the cousin who had drifted out of her life on her marriage to Hugh Waring.

Sylvie had promptly fallen in love with the beautiful old house, so impressively set amid the hills with superb views of one of the loveliest lakes in Cumbria.

Her suite of rooms overlooked the Hall's own lake and the formal gardens and, in the distance, the small copse that made up part of its many lovely acres. Used to the rugged countryside and coastline of Cornwall, she was captivated by the rolling splendours of the Lake District and she had enjoyed her first few days, exploring, sketching, delighting in her new surroundings.

But now Edward had arrived to spoil all her pleasure, she thought with a little resentment, knowing that she disliked him and the woman he had brought with him . . .

Maude Carluke looked up from her tapestry work as the trio entered her sitting-room. For some years, she had been embroidering the saga of Carluke family history with skilful fingers and a faultless eye for blending her colours. In due course, it was destined to hang on the wall.

"There you are, my dear — " She broke off and her still-lovely face brightened at sight of her beloved son. "Edward! I didn't expect you today! How very nice!" She gave him her hand and he carried it to his lips, smiling down at her with an affection and a tender warmth that redeemed him just a little in Sylvie's eyes. She had become very fond of Cousin Maude in the few days that she had known her . . .

"You're looking well, Mama," Edward approved.

"I feel so much better since Sylvie arrived. I like young people about the place, as you know. She's quite charming, too. But you've met Sylvie, made yourselves known to each other, I see . . ." She beamed on them both.

"Yes," he said briefly. He drew Diantha forward. "Mama, I've brought someone with me that I know you have long wished to meet . . . Diantha Craig. Diantha, Mama is a great admirer of your books."

Maude's bright eyes looked with interest at the beautiful and very gifted woman. She had heard through friends that she was Edward's latest *amour*.

It was her dearest wish that her son should marry and settle down and give her grandchildren . . . and she had few years left. At thirty-one, he showed no sign of complying with that wish. There were far too many women in his life and most of them were quite unsuited to be his wife and the mistress of Chase Hall.

This woman was different. She was lovely, dressed in the height of fashion, very sure of herself. She was a woman of means, used to moving in the best circles. She would be a very good wife for Edward, no doubt. Maude knew instinctively that she had every intention of persuading Edward into marriage. It was a pity that she could not like her. Perhaps she was just disappointed. She had set her heart on the pretty Sylvie for a daughter-in-law and she was not only swayed by Hugh Waring's millions. She had become very fond of poor Frances' girl in a very short time.

However, Edward had gone his own way for years and the merest suspicion that she had chosen a bride for him would put him against the girl . . .

The tea-tray arrived and Sylvie busied herself with pouring tea, handing sandwiches and delicate cakes with her shy, rather sweet smile, taking little part in the conversation. She might have been the daughter of the house and certainly Cousin Maude had treated her with motherly affection and a comfortable ease ever since she had arrived at the Hall. Secure in that kindliness, it could not really matter that Edward Carluke virtually ignored her or that Diantha Craig treated her with an air of patronizing indulgence.

Sylvie studied the novelist. She knew little about writers but suspected that they were seldom the glamorous beings of public imagination. Diantha Craig was glamorous, however. Her clothes probably came from the most expensive couturiers and her hair was probably styled by the most famous coiffeurs,

Sylvie decided. She wore the most modern make-up, skilfully applied, and expensive perfume wafted on the air whenever she turned that lovely head. It seemed that she knew everyone, too. She chatted easily of people and places that were mere names to Sylvie . . . minor royalties, celebrities of stage and screen, writers and journalists, politicians and a number of men and women who frequently figured in the social columns of national newspapers.

It was the world that Lady Carluke had known and loved until failing health forced her into the quiet, retired life of a semi-invalid. It was a world of which Sylvie knew next to nothing.

Her father had determined that she should not be a spoiled darling of society because of his wealth. She had grown up in a quiet corner of Cornwall with very little awareness of his fame as a financier with his finger in many political pies. She had gone to schools that were noted for academic achievements rather than famous pupils and received a sound if narrow education. She had travelled with her parents, staying in all the right places without meeting any of the right people. Her father disliked the bright lights and sophistication of the social scene and avoided it as much as possible. Sylvie's life had been filled with simple pleasures — reading and sketching, riding, walking the dogs, swimming and sailing, her love of music.

Her mother had died just when Sylvie should have emerged into society as a pretty and personable young woman, making friends of her own age and preparing for eventual marriage with a little, light-hearted flirtation. As a result of her mother's death and her father's reclusive habits when he was not advising various political leaders on the nation's economy, she had met very few eligible men and had a very narrow social life.

Every girl had her dreams and Sylvie dreamed of a handsome knight on a white charger who would sweep into her life and carry her off to the world of romantic love and happy ever after. In her dreams, he was usually as fair as herself with classical good looks and blue eyes and a ready smile, blessed with all the excellent qualities that a girl looked for in a husband. In her dreams, he fell in love at first sight and overcame all kinds of opposition from her father and his family to marry her.

It was true that sometimes, a little bored with her gentil parfait knight, she toyed with a dream that featured the dark-haired and very sensual Edward Carluke, careless lover of so many women, fancying him swept off his feet into real and lasting love at the first glimpse of her blonde loveliness. Now, recalling the foolish fantasy, a smile quivered as she glanced at him and remembered their clash at first meeting. She did not like him. It was obvious that she had not made a very favourable impression on him.

So much for dreams . . .

Edward lounged in a chair, long legs stretched before him, hands deep in his pockets. He had ceased to listen to the eager exchange between his mother and Diantha. He had known that they would take to each other for they had much in common. He was very sure that his mother would approve if he decided to marry the writer. Now, with a faintly sardonic gleam in his dark eyes, he was studying the girl who was studying Diantha with such frank curiosity.

She was a mere child in comparison with the sophisticated and very worldly Diantha . . . a fair, wide-eyed child with an innocence about her that struck him as most unusual in this day and age. Sylvie Waring. The name was unfamiliar to him. But the family tree had many branches. He knew little about his mother's side and cared less. He knew a great deal about the Carlukes and tried in vain to remember which of them had married a Waring.

18

Sylvie. It was a pretty name. And she was a pretty thing with that pale hair and flawless skin, untouched by make-up, the shining grey eyes with that sweeping fan of long, dark lashes. The frock she was wearing did not do justice to a slight but very shapely figure. Bare arms and slender legs were sun-kissed and she had the healthy glow of the outdoor girl.

She was very different to most of the women he knew, he mused idly . . . and then interest abruptly quickened as she glanced at him with unmistakable, dancing amusement in the depths of those grey eyes. It was fleeting, gone in a moment, but it intrigued him. For what did she find in him to amuse her so much? he wondered.

There had been no trace of coquetry in that glance. He fancied that she did not know how to flirt. Unlike most women that he met, she had not made the least attempt to attract his notice and she seemed utterly unaware of his scrutiny. She sat quietly, like a well-behaved child, outwardly attentive to the conversation and the needs of the company but really intent on her own thoughts. For some reason, he had figured in those thoughts — and not to his advantage, he fancied, a little amused.

"When did you arrive, Miss Waring?" he asked, deciding to draw her out.

"Last Thursday." She turned to him with cool, dutiful courtesy.

He nodded. "And how long are we to have the pleasure of your company?"

The grey eyes were suddenly sceptical and he was delighted by her dislike of polite conversation. Perhaps she was not very used to people who said one thing while meaning something very different.

There was something about the girl that was refreshing — and his palate was very jaded. It might be amusing to teach this unworldly child some of the facts of life. And Diantha was becoming too sure of herself — and of him. It might not be a bad thing to shake her confidence slightly.

"I'm not sure . . . a few weeks," Sylvie said briefly. She doubted that he expected to find any pleasure in her company. She was nothing like the women in his life. He would be bored by her lack of conversation, her lack of familiarity with his world and his way of life, her lack of all that made someone like Diantha Craig so attractive to him.

She did not want him to seek her company. She wanted to be free to enjoy herself in her own way, going for long walks, riding, swimming and sunbathing, reading and sketching, playing the piano and talking contentedly to his mother of the days when she had been a girl with her own mother.

Lady Carluke intervened, leaving a lively and slightly scandalous discussion of a mutual friend. "Surely there's no need to be so formal," she said brightly. "Edward, you've heard me speak of my cousin Frances many times. She married Hugh Waring, you will recall. Sylvie is their daughter. Quite one of the family — and I hope that she will spend the rest of the summer with us." She smiled warmly and leaned to pat Sylvie's hand. "We've had a very happy few days together, haven't we, my dear?"

Edward saw the swift response in the girl's smile and recognized genuine liking and affection for his mother.

Hugh Waring's daughter! No wonder his mother was as bright as a button! She was a born optimist and no doubt she believed that she had only to throw them together for a few weeks to achieve her obvious desire of bringing about his marriage to the girl! He wondered if Sylvie knew what was in his mother's mind. She might be very young and very inexperienced but he did not think that she was a fool. Perhaps she was a willing party to the scheme, he thought dryly.

Hugh Waring's daughter! Surely his mother did not really suppose he would marry any girl for the sake of her father's enormous wealth! At the same time, his heroic efforts to keep the lovely Hall and its surrounding acres had taken him deeply into debt. He loved his home and his land and he knew he would go to almost any lengths to keep it intact for his eventual heir.

No one realized more clearly than Edward Carluke that he needed to marry for money as much as for an heir to his title and estates. Her cousin's daughter, young and persuadable, must seem like a gift from heaven to his optimistic mother. But he knew that marriage to such a shy innocent was out of the question. The girl would be completely out of place in his world.

Hugh Waring's daughter! Damn it, a man could be sorely tempted . . .

Diantha looked at the girl she had virtually ignored with a new interest. So that was Hugh Waring's girl, heiress to a vast fortune! Everyone had heard of her but she had been kept so much in the background that no one knew very much about her. She was not in the least like Hugh. Perhaps she resembled her mother, the wife that Hugh had guarded so jealously through the years. His private life had been very private, she knew. He was an eccentric man but he had a brilliant mind and a great deal of influence in important circles. And he was a financial wizard.

It was the first she had heard of a family connection between the Carlukes and the wealthy Hugh Waring. It was really rather distant and Diantha suspected that Maude Carluke had forgotten all about her 'dear cousin Frances' until it occurred to her that the Waring girl was of marriageable age.

Everyone knew that Edward was in financial difficulties and needed to marry money. Sylvie Waring was young and probably persuadable — and she might not know about his rather wild reputation or his inability to be faithful to any woman for long.

Her own days were probably numbered,

Diantha felt, but it did not please her that she might lose him to an unsophisticated girl with little to recommend her but the fact that she was Hugh Waring's daughter . . .

Observing the changing expressions in that handsome, sensual face, Sylvie decided that she would not be surprised if Edward Carluke revised his first impression and began to pay her some attention. Being her father's daughter, she was far from stupid and very level-headed . . . and she suspected that his mother would have a quiet and very urgent word in his ear in the very near future.

For while she felt that Maude Carluke was becoming genuinely attached to her, she realized that her elderly cousin also regarded her as a possible solution to the financial problems that beset her beloved son.

And, noting that flicker of interest in Diantha Craig's lovely face at the mention of her famous father's name, Sylvie wondered if the woman suddenly saw her as a threat. Perhaps she had her own plans for Edward!

Protected by her father's loving concern, it was Sylvie's first taste of the disillusion that could accompany the possession of great wealth. Her heart suddenly sank as she wondered whether even the splendid hero of her youthful dreams, if he appeared suddenly in her life, might be influenced by mercenary ambition rather than true love . . .

# 2

SYLVIE dawdled in the bath and spent a long time kneeling on the window-seat in her pretty sitting-room with a thin silk robe wrapped about her slender body, admiring the splendour of the scenery in the setting sun.

The rain had cleared and it was a lovely evening and she ought to be dressing for dinner. Several people were expected for Edward had been busy telephoning various friends and his mother had declared indulgently that he loved to fill the house with people.

Sylvie was reluctant to go down and wished she had a valid excuse for dining in her room. She was not used to meeting a lot of strangers and she was nervous of meeting the kind of friends that Edward had

27

obviously invited . . . women like Diantha Craig and men like himself. She hoped that Lady Carluke would refrain from introducing her to all and sundry as 'Hugh Waring's daughter' and thought it unlikely.

With a little sigh, she moved away from the window and went into her bedroom. She threw off her robe and reached for the flimsy underthings that lay across the bed. Being a modest girl, she gave little thought to the perfection of small, tilting breasts and slender waist and narrow hips, of long and lovely legs.

She donned an expensive silk jersey dress of old gold that clung to every curve of her body and she wound her long hair in a crown of plaits about her shapely head. It was a quaintly old-fashioned style but it suited her very well. When it came to jewellery, she hesitated. She had some lovely pieces but she hated to parade her father's wealth. She settled for a simple gold chain about her neck and matching studs for her ears and, as always, she wore her mother's favourite ring on her right hand, a diamond sunburst.

She met Edward on the stairs. He paused at sight of her and she saw a swift flicker of real admiration in his dark eyes. She was satisfied — and only then did she admit that she had taken pains with her appearance in order to impress a man who was always surrounded by beautiful women.

Sylvie knew very well that she was far from beautiful. But there were moments when she felt that she might be pretty — and that was one of them!

Edward looked very handsome in a midnight blue dinner jacket and pale blue frilled evening shirt, open at the neck in the current fashion to reveal the bronzed column of his throat and the heavy gold chain that he was wearing. His dark hair was crisp and waving, the white streak standing out vividly.

He smiled . . . and Sylvie foolishly felt her heart give a little jump. She would need to be very stern with herself to resist the physical attractions of this man, she realized.

"I was just coming to find you," he said.

"But I'm not lost," she returned calmly.

Edward laughed. He held his hand out as though they were friends. "You look delightful — like a little girl dressed up in her mother's clothes! Come and meet my friends."

Sylvie did not know whether to be pleased or infuriated by a compliment that was no compliment at all. It was pleasing to be told that she looked delightful — and infuriating that she had been reminded that she looked ridiculously young no matter what she did! She had that kind of face, she thought bitterly — unstamped with any degree of the maturity that comes with experience!

Pretending not to see that outstretched hand, she sailed down the remaining stairs with a dignity that only caused his smile to deepen with amusement.

She was really rather an appealing chit, Edward told himself, escorting her across the hall and into the drawing-room.

Lady Carluke was holding court as in days of old, sparkling, animated. The room was filled with people, most of them Edward's friends but a few invited to amuse and entertain his mother. Sylvie recognized a face here and there, having met some of Lady Carluke's friends and neighbours since her arrival at the Hall.

Suddenly unsure of herself, she hesitated on the threshold of the big room. She found Edward's hand at her elbow and she glanced up to meet the warm, reassuring smile in his eyes. She liked him in that moment — and then reminded herself that it would not do to like him too much. She knew all about his dangerous reputation. He was fickle and heartless and much too attractive for his own good or anyone else's, she told herself firmly.

That momentary hesitation had the effect of turning most eyes towards them. A murmur rippled round the room and one or two eyebrows were raised. Edward increased the pressure on her arm and urged her forward.

Diantha, dressed in a clinging, low-cut black dinner dress, was talking brightly to a very tall, fair man with a pleasant smile and very blue eyes in a tanned, intelligent face. She broke off in mid-sentence as Edward took Sylvie across the room to join them.

Sylvie wondered if the woman had been telling her companion to be nice to 'Hugh Waring's daughter' and release Edward from the dreary task of looking after her that evening. As she was his mother's guest, he was duty-bound to do so, she suddenly realized with a little dismay. She had stupidly supposed that an unsuspected kindness had led him to take a shy and obviously unsophisticated girl under his wing.

Her suspicion was confirmed by the man's warmth and friendliness of manner when they were introduced. Leo Bryce was a near neighbour and a close friend of the family, it seemed. He had also been acquainted for some years with Diantha Craig and had first introduced her to Edward. He was very good-looking and he had a great deal of easy charm — and a talent for putting shy people immediately at their ease, Sylvie discovered, warming to him.

"But I've seen you several times," he told her lightly, very friendly. "You're a great walker, aren't you?"

"I like to walk," she agreed, smiling. "And there are so many lovely places to explore in this corner of England."

"You were exploring my small corner early this morning. In fact, we passed each other, you know. I wanted to speak to you but you seemed so wrapped in thought that it would have seemed an intrusion, I felt."

"Oh, dear — was I trespassing?" she said quickly, rather ruefully. "I thought I might be. Hero went through a gap in the fence and I couldn't resist the temptation to explore the woods. They are very beautiful."

"You may trespass whenever you wish and welcome," Leo assured her, smiling. "I don't mend the fence because Edward usually walks through the woods instead of taking the longer route by road to Rylands. I'm glad you like our lovely Cumbria, Miss Waring. Where do you live, by the way?"

"Cornwall, near Penzance . . . and please — call me Sylvie, won't you?" she said, a little shy.

"Then you must call me Leo — and that makes us friends." He smiled at her warmly.

She found him beside her at dinner. Chance — or planning? she wondered. He was very attentive in the quiet, unassuming way that put her so much at ease. She did not think that Lady Carluke was too pleased that they were getting on so well or that Edward was taking very little notice of her. But she was too clever to make it obvious.

Edward was being monopolized by

Diantha on one side and a very pretty girl on the other who turned out to be Leo Bryce's sister Lucinda.

It took Sylvie some time to sort everybody out, putting the right names to faces . . . and more people arrived later in the evening. There was conversation and music and then dancing was suggested and rugs rolled up and furniture hastily pushed into corners of the big room.

Lady Carluke took her cronies off to her sitting-room for a quiet game of bridge. Lucinda began to sort through a pile of records. Edward went around the room replenishing glasses, playing the part of dutiful and courteous host.

It was a sultry evening. Not wishing to dance, Sylvie slipped out to the terrace, glad of the cool night air on her face and hair. Her head was swimming slightly from the wine at dinner and the drinks that followed.

She leaned against the stone parapet, glad to be alone for a few moments. She felt a little shy, overwhelmed by so many strangers. She was out of her depth, she knew, unable to hold her own in sophisticated banter, the confident references to a social calender about which she knew little, the light and rather scurrilous gossip about people who were merely names.

It was enchanting to stand in the moonlight that bathed the terrace and the formal gardens in an eerie beauty and reflected off the lake in the distance. The music in the background suited her mood, too . . . soft, romantic and full of dreams.

Suddenly she became aware of a couple who danced close by, moving sensually to the music. It was impossible to mistake those curls, gleaming in the moonlight, or that proud head and that clear, carrying voice. Diantha danced with Leo Bryce, their bodies melting very close.

Sylvie drew into the shadows cast by the bulk of the house — and collided with Edward who stood behind her, observing her slender figure with a thoughtful gleam in his dark eyes.

He steadied her, smiled down at her as she murmured an apology. "You're an introspective young woman," he said lightly. "Why aren't you dancing? Don't you dance?"

She shook her head. "Not very well." Not with all those hostile eyes on me, she thought dryly, everyone wondering if he means to marry me!

"I'm sure that isn't true. You have a natural rhythm in the way that you move. I've noticed." He reached for her hand. "Dance with me, Sylvie."

She resisted. "I'd rather not . . . "

The smile in the dark eyes deepened. "Women don't say no to me, you know," he said smoothly, very confident.

"More's the pity, perhaps," she returned, tart, disliking the conceit in his words.

Edward laughed. "I daresay." He put an arm about her, drew her towards him. "Dance with me," he repeated with just the hint of command in his tone.

Sylvie stood very still, tense and a little angry, refusing to move with the music, the urging of his body. She was rather startled to discover that she quickened with an odd excitement at his touch, his nearness . . . or was it the sudden intent in those dark and much too attractive eyes?

Edward was challenged by the involuntary shrinking of her slight body in his embrace. Her shyness and her obvious inexperience held a considerable appeal for him, he found.

"Stubborn wench," he said softly. "How can you resist the combination of the night and the music — and me!" There was gentle self-mockery in his tone that coaxed her to laugh with him.

"I wish you would let me go." Sylvie was quiet but firm. She knew it would be undignified to struggle with him and he was obviously too strong for her to escape the cage of his arms. But she did not like what was happening to her as she stood in his embrace. He was really much too attractive, too exciting . . .

Edward was surprised by her composure. Women usually melted into his arms at the first sign of his interest. This girl was different. She did not seem at all touched by the physical magnetism that usually proved so potent.

There had been many women in his life but not one quite like this girl, he realized. He was enchanted by her youthful prettiness, her modesty, her air of innocence. She was refreshingly different to all the other women he had known. He marvelled that he had been so ready to dismiss her at first sight. Now he knew that he was irresistibly drawn by this slight, shy and very appealing girl.

"Not yet." His arms tightened about her and he laid his cheek against the soft, pale hair. "I've been aching to kiss you since I saw you coming down the stairs this evening . . . a little girl suddenly grown up," he said urgently.

His lips were on her hair, at her temple, straying lightly down her cheek towards her mouth. Sylvie's heart began to pound and it was suddenly very difficult to breathe. A little tremor of delight ran through her slight body, shocking her with that swift and unexpected response to him.

She jerked her head as his lips touched, hovered against her own. "No . . . !"

Disregarding that instinctive protest, he kissed her . . . gently at first and then with growing ardour. His arms were very tight about her and her soft breasts were crushed against that hard chest. Sylvie found herself drowning in an unsuspected flood of yearning. For the first time, she knew desire, found herself aching for his touch on her breast, a closer and more intimate contact with this man. For the first time, she understood the powerful force of a passion that could excite and demand and transport her to a new and wonderful world . . . and it troubled her that such fire could leap between two people who were virtual strangers and had no thought of loving.

Men were very different, she knew . . . but surely she ought not to want Edward Carluke with such a fierce and frightening flame!

He kissed her and her mouth quivered just a little beneath his lips. But she fought down the urge to respond as he obviously expected. She was quiescent and seemingly unmoved in his embrace until he raised his head.

For a moment, he continued to hold her, very close. "Sylvie . . . " he said, very tense. "Sylvie . . . " It was a sigh, a soft murmur, a breath of wonder on his lips. Never again would she think it a name without charm.

As his hold relaxed, she stepped out of his arms. "Don't ever do that again," she said quietly, coldly. She despised herself more than him. For it was the height of folly to be so moved by a man who had no respect for any woman and had too many conquests to his credit.

"Kiss you against your will? No, my sweet innocent." He smiled, a little mischief in his eyes. "Next time you'll want me as much as I want you," he told her and it was a promise.

Her chin tilted. "There won't be a next time!" But, being a woman, she could not help a little leap of satisfaction that he had found pleasure in kissing her and wished to do it again.

Edward would not accept that he might be denied the joy of holding her, kissing her, delighting in her warm, sweet femininity. He had never been thwarted in his pursuit of a woman. He wanted this girl as he had never wanted any woman. If needs must, he would marry her, he decided — and regard her father's wealth as a bonus!

"I'm not going to apologize," he said lightly. "How can I be sorry that I kissed you? It would be no compliment to you if I were! Now . . . will you dance with me?" He held out a hand.

"I will not!"

He laughed. "Don't trust me! Very well. I shall dance with Diantha and you'll hate me for it!"

Sylvie looked at him coldly. "You're the most conceited man I've ever met," she said, turning away . . . and the sound of his laughter followed her as she crossed the terrace.

She meant to go to her room, needing more than ever to be alone to marshal her tumbled thoughts and emotions. For while she did not like Edward Carluke very much; her foolish body responded to his physical attractions and she knew that her treacherous heart stirred with a strange excitement because of him.

Leo Bryce moved to intercept her, having surrendered Diantha to another man . . . the story of his life, he told himself wryly.

But why should the lovely and clever and very successful Diantha want a mere farmer like himself? He had little to offer but his love — and she had been loved by many men and refused them all. Now he thought that she meant to marry Edward and it was ironic that he had introduced her to his friend. But Edward might prove to be elusive. He was in no hurry to marry while he could enjoy the company and the charms of any woman he fancied.

Leo was surprised that he seemed to fancy the shy girl who was Lady Carluke's guest. Some kind of family connection, apparently. She was very young and a little shy and obviously inexperienced . . . not at all Edward's type as a rule, he thought cynically, knowing his friend very well.

He liked Sylvie Waring. She had a sweet smile and an appealing modesty and there was something about her youth and slight build and retiring ways that evoked a man's chivalrous feelings. He wondered if he ought to warn her against taking Edward's attentions at all seriously — and against his friend's rakish tendencies. Lady Carluke was naturally blind to her son's faults.

Someone ought to give an eye to the girl, Leo thought, a trifle anxiously.

Sylvie smiled at him. The turmoil within her slowly subsided as they stood together on the terrace, talking with the ease of friendship. She felt as though she had always known this man. He was nice, reassuring, comfortable to be with. He was very tall, so tall that her head barely reached his shoulder. His fair hair shone silver in the moonlight. He had the type of regular good looks that would scarcely alter with age. He would never cause her pulses to quicken, she knew. But she felt that he would be a good and reliable friend if she should need one.

"It's a beautiful night," she said, a little dreamily. "Just look at that moon." Very full, enormous in the night sky, sailing proudly overhead through mere wisps of cloud.

"Rather surprising after such a wet day," Leo remarked.

She nodded. "Sometimes the whole world seems lovelier after rain, don't you think? Fresh and clean and wholesome . . . a new beginning. Life can be like that, too."

She was not such a child as she seemed, Leo thought, intrigued. "You are too young to know about new beginnings, surely," he said gently. "And I hope you will have very little rain in your life."

Impulsively she put a hand through his arm. "Clever of you to know what was in my mind!"

"Oh, I'm a clever chap for a farmer," he told her, smiling.

Sylvie laughed. "Will you show me over your farm? Is it very big?"

"More acres than you would wish to walk in a day. But you ride, I know. Come to lunch tomorrow and I'll provide you with a sweet-mouthed mare who'll give you a splendid ride over the hills."

"I'd like that very much . . ."

Diantha linked both hands about Edward's neck as she danced with him, her body swaying provocatively, steps matching perfectly. "Your little cousin seems to have made a conquest," she said lightly, having overheard Leo's friendly offer. "Leo doesn't let just anyone ride his beloved horses."

"She's an appealing child," he returned carelessly. "My mother seems to have taken to her, too. She needed an interest and Sylvie seems to have supplied it."

Diantha's eyes hardened slightly. She was not so easily taken in by that youthful simplicity, that demure innocence. She suspected that Sylvie Waring was in league with Lady Carluke to lure Edward into marriage. He was a very attractive man, a baronet of ancient lineage and extensive estate. Hugh Waring would no doubt consider him an excellent husband for his daughter — and Edward would be well rewarded with a handsome settlement.

The girl knew perfectly well what she was about as she encouraged Leo to take an interest in her, Diantha decided. She knew that her father's wealth was a considerable attraction. Her pretty face and figure was another for a man of Edward's sensual nature. Leo's attentiveness and her own pretence of indifference to him would certainly draw Edward's interest for he could never resist that kind of challenge. It all made for a combination that could be dangerous, thought Diantha, determined to be on her guard. She had her own plans for Edward's future and it was very much linked with her own!

"Leo only means to be kind, of course," she said airily. "Girls of that age are not much in his line. Wide-eyed innocence palls very quickly when a man is used to mature women. But at least he will take her off your hands to some extent, darling."

"She isn't on my hands," Edward told her lightly. "Sylvie is my mother's guest."

Diantha's smile was knowing. "Your mother is well aware that she is dull company for someone so young. Naturally she looked to you to entertain

48

the girl once you were home. She makes me very welcome but I do feel she is rather vexed with you for bringing me here, darling. Sylvie Waring was invited for a very good reason and you chose quite the wrong moment to throw a spanner in the works!"

He laughed. "And such a beautiful spanner, too! Poor Mama!"

"She is much too young for you, of course," Diantha declared confidently. "Girls of that age are not to your taste, either."

A little devil lurked in his dark eyes. "Sure of that, are you?"

"No," she said promptly, wisely.

Edward chuckled softly. "Clever as well as beautiful," he approved. Someone called him and he kissed her briefly and broke away. When he returned a few minutes later, Diantha was talking to Leo and his sister. Edward looked about him for Sylvie. There was no sign of her on the terrace or in the sunken garden.

He went in search of the girl

and met her as she came out of his mother's sitting-room. "I thought you'd run away," he said lightly.

Sylvie was surprised that he had missed her. She had thought him wholly preoccupied with Diantha Craig and told herself firmly that it was better that way for all concerned.

"I've been saying my goodnights."

"You aren't going to bed, surely! The night is still young," he protested. "And you still haven't danced with me."

She smiled coolly. "You are used to late hours. I'm not."

He put a hand beneath her chin and tilted the small face. She stiffened. "You don't look at all tired. Bored? Disappointed? Don't you like my friends?"

Sylvie moved away from that disturbing touch. "Everyone has been very nice to me," she said fairly.

"Even me," he said, smiling. "And Leo in particular, I've noticed. Like him, do you?"

"Very much." Her voice was warm.

"Your father won't approve," Edward told her, amusement crinkling his dark eyes. "No title and not very much land."

Colour swept into her face. "You're impossible!" she snapped. "Do you really think I would marry a man my father chose for me?"

He did not answer immediately. Then: "I think you might . . . if I were to ask you," he said outrageously.

Sylvie caught her breath. "You flatter yourself!" she said tartly — and hoped that hc would never ask her to marry him. For she might be terribly tempted to say yes!

Life with Edward Carluke would probably be exciting and interesting and full of adventure, vastly different to the quiet and sheltered life she had always known. He was nothing like the gentle, courteous knight of her youthful dreams. But hadn't she often found *him* just a little boring?

51

# 3

SYLVIE ate breakfast in solitary state.

Lady Carluke always had a tray in her room and seldom rose before eleven o'clock. There was no sign of Edward or Diantha Craig who had obviously gone to bed very much later than herself.

She felt just a little reluctant to meet Edward that morning, remembering the provocative words of the previous night. She burned with indignation that he should have assumed with such arrogant conceit that she would leap at a proposal of marriage from him. Nothing would induce her to marry him for any reason at all, she told herself firmly. A man with his reputation would be a very bad husband even if he loved his wife, she felt. As the husband of a woman he married merely for money, she would never know comfort or peace of mind or the slightest happiness!

Simply because he had kissed her, entirely against her will, he seemed to think that she found him attractive. She went quite cold at the thought that he might have sensed the instinctive response that she had tried so hard to conceal.

Determined to keep out of his way as much as possible, Sylvie left the house soon after breakfast, heading for the lake. It promised to be a hot day and there was plenty of time to swim and to relax in the sunshine before she would need to get ready for lunch with the Bryces. Over her swimsuit she wore a white sundress. The long, pale blonde hair was kept away from her face by a wide white ribbon and she wore white sandals on her bare feet. She took a book and her sketching things with her for amusement.

She was a distinctive figure as she crossed the trim lawns and Edward, taking his first look at the new day from his bedroom window, smiled with swift appreciation. He decided that a swim before breakfast would dispel his heavy-eyed lethargy and give him an appetite. And he welcomed the opportunity to further his acquaintance with Sylvie Waring . . .

The lake was small in comparison with the famous lakes of the district. But it was clean and clear and a lovely jewel in its beautiful setting. Sylvie swam well, having lived by the sea all her life, and the water, surprisingly cold, was exhilarating. She did not see Edward's approach and she was unaware that he stood for some minutes at the edge of the lake, watching her, before he slipped into the water and swam beneath its surface to emerge suddenly beside her, startling her, his dark hair sleeked to his handsome head and his dark eyes laughing into her own.

Sylvie was annoyed by his intrusion into an idyll . . . or perhaps she was just annoyed with herself for being pleased to see him, returning his smile quite involuntarily. On such a lovely morning and in such perfect surroundings, it was difficult to remember that she was cross with him.

"Hallo . . . !" he exclaimed in mock surprise. "You're a lovely mermaid to find in my lake. I've been looking for you for years!"

"I expect you say that to every mermaid you happen to meet," Sylvie returned lightly . . . and swam away with a grace and a turn of speed that surprised him.

She found him swimming effortlessly by her side, the powerful arms cleaving through the water. She could not help admiring his style and his strength. She paused, trod water, watching him as he swam to the far end of the lake. He turned, came back, dived deep and came up very close to her, his hands running lightly up the long legs to the slender waist and lingering with intent. Sylvie wriggled out of his grasp . . . and sped for the shore, laughing. He followed. She eluded him several times for he was not trying very hard to catch her. They frolicked like a couple of children in the cool water and Sylvie briefly forgot that she did not like him.

She escaped him, looked back over her shoulder, laughing and breathless, and saw no sign of him. She knew he must be swimming under water and looked about her warily. She was just beginning to be anxious, wondering if he were entangled in unsuspected weeds below the water, when he emerged, shaking the water from his hair and eyes. He saw the undisguised relief in her wide grey eyes. He grinned. "Did you think I'd drowned?"

"Of course not . . . " she began stoutly.

"You *were* worried," he teased gently. "My sweet, I know this lake like the back of my hand. There are one or two treacherous parts and that's why I came to join you. I like to look after my guests . . . especially the pretty ones."

"I'm getting chilled," she said abruptly. She swam towards the shore and he accompanied her, took her hand to draw her from the water and help her up to the grassy bank. She saw the swift, appraising glance that flickered over her body in the clinging wet swimsuit. She recognized the dawning of desire in the dark eyes and felt her face grow hot and her heart quicken with mingled apprehension and excitement.

Edward reached for a towel and draped it about her slim shoulders, keeping hold of the ends — and then he drew her towards him, smiling, a little imp of mischief in the depths of his eyes. Sylvie resisted, conscious of the maleness of that lithe and powerful body, so close to her own. Her heart leaped in sudden alarm.

"Don't spoil things!" she exclaimed warmly, trying to push him away with her hands on his bronzed chest.

"I'm trying to improve things," he

said softly. "Our relationship, for instance . . . "

"I'd rather you didn't!"

His arms enfolded her abruptly, with intent. "Don't you like to be kissed, Sylvie?" His voice caressed her name, softly and seductively.

"Not by you." She lied because her heart was thudding like a wild thing against her ribs and she was terrified that she might betray the leaping response in her blood if their lips met.

"You don't approve of my technique . . . is that it?" he teased gently. "You're an expert in such matters, I daresay." He smiled into the grey eyes, so wide, so obviously apprehensive. He was touched by her alarm, born of an innocence he had not met in a very long time. He did not mean her any harm, of course. It was not his practice to go about seducing virgins. He only wanted a few kisses, the delight of a brief titillation that would not seek to be satisfied in her embrace.

Sylvie thought that he knew very well

that she was an absolute novice in the game of flirtation. It was unkind of him to take advantage of that fact, she felt. She could not help being physically aware of him to an extent that frightened her. It had nothing to do with like or dislike, apparently, much to her surprise. She did not know how to cope with the feelings that he aroused in her but she knew better than to yield to them. It was unfair that he should pursue her in this way when he was only amusing himself because her inexperience was a novelty, she thought angrily.

"I'm a guest in your house," she reminded him sharply. "You're making my position intolerable by forcing yourself on me. I thought you were a gentleman!" Her tone was contemptuous.

Edward laughed, amused by the old-fashioned reproach. "By birth but not by nature, I'm afraid . . . not if it means denying myself the pleasure of kissing someone as delightful as you, my sweet.

No don't struggle!" he added sharply, his arms tightening almost painfully about her slender body. "Because you'll get hurt — and I don't want to hurt you, Sylvie. One kiss and I'll let you go!" He was determined not to be thwarted.

"Very well," she said coldly, doubting him, despising him. She raised her face like an obedient child.

He knew that her lips would be as cold and as unresponsive as the last time. That was not what he wanted. He released her abruptly, disappointed and a little angry. Perhaps his reputation did not encourage her to trust him. But he was a man of honour and a man of his word.

He threw himself down on the grass and stretched out in the sun, eyes closed, a rather forbidding tightness about his sensual mouth. Sylvie looked down at him, hesitant. It was foolish to feel guilty because she had rebuffed him. After all, it was only a game to him.

She picked up the towel that had fallen to the ground from her shoulders and rubbed a little half-heartedly at the wet hair that streamed down her back, darkened by dampness. She felt oddly wretched. She had wanted him to kiss her, of course — far too much for comfort. What was the matter with her that she found him so attractive when she scarcely knew him and hardly liked him? Most of the time, she disliked and despised him. It was only in moments of foolish weakness that she melted towards him, ached for his kiss, his touch, his embrace. She understood why women fell for him so easily. He was a charmer when he wished to be. He was the most handsome man she had ever known. He had a forceful physical magnetism that drew her against all reason and all discretion.

He was annoyed. Well, didn't all men hate to be rebuffed and he was apparently a man of very strong desires. Remembering the latent passion she had sensed in him when he held her close to him, she could not help wondering if he would have been content with a mere kiss . . . and she might have been too weak to resist him once their lips met and held, she thought wryly. They were out of sight and sound of the house, screened by trees . . . and she was so scantily clad that any man might be fired with desire and eager to make the most of an opportunity to make love to her. And Edward Carluke was reputed to be more of an opportunist than most!

He did not look like the heartless rake of the stories that were circulated about him. With eyes closed against the bright sun, arms outflung in seeming abandon and his expression softening as he relaxed, he looked younger than his years and almost vulnerable. Sylvie's heart gave an odd little lurch. In that moment, she felt very drawn to him — and it had nothing to do with his marked sensuality.

On an impulse, she reached for her

sketchbook and pencil and sank down to the grass some little distance from him. With a few skilful strokes, she had captured him to her satisfaction. Her head bent over the pad, she did not realize that he was observing her thoughtfully.

Edward rolled on to his stomach and stretched out his hand. "What's that? Show me . . ."

Sylvie hesitated. Then she put the pad into his hand. She had no need to blush for her sketches. She knew them to be good. It was one of her very few accomplishments and it gave her a great deal of pleasure.

Edward studied the sketch of himself with an enigmatic expression. Then he said, not too pleased: "You make me look like a sulky boy."

Sylvie smiled. "Weren't you sulking?" she challenged him gently.

He scowled. "I should bloody well hope not! I don't give a damn if you kiss me or not, my sweet. There are plenty who will!"

She was taken aback by the sudden violence in his tone. She held out her hand for her sketching pad. "Please . . . " There was a heightened colour in her small face, a little discomfiture in her grey eyes.

"Not yet." He turned the pages, lingering at an excellent sketch of his mother at her tapestry work. "You have talent," he said shortly.

"Thank you."

"And a touch of malice," he said abruptly, coming across a sketch of Diantha that had captured her beauty and also a somewhat feline self-satisfaction. "When did you do this?"

"Last night," she admitted.

Edward nodded. "Don't like her, do you?"

Sylvie shrugged. "Must I?"

"No. But I don't advise you to allow this drawing to fall into her hands," he said, tapping the page, a smile glinting in his dark eyes. "She can be a dangerous enemy."

Sylvie looked at him in surprise.

"How could she possibly harm me?"

"She'd find a way," he said grimly.

Sylvie shrugged. "There is little risk that she'll see that drawing," she said lightly. "I never show my sketches."

"Then I am honoured," he said carelessly, tossing the book into her lap.

"Just arrogant," she amended tartly. "You didn't give me much choice."

Edward laughed, his ill-humour banished. "You're enchanting!" he declared warmly. "I might marry you yet."

"And you might not!" she retorted, ignoring the little start of her heart. "I'm not looking for a husband."

He raised an eyebrow, sceptical. "Then what are you doing here?" he asked bluntly.

"Getting to know my long-lost relatives — and not liking them very much," she said coolly.

He smiled. "I thought you liked my Mama."

"I do. I can almost forgive her for

having a son like you. I'm sure it wasn't intentional," Sylvie said sweetly.

His dark eyes danced. "I take after my late and not very lamented father."

"It does you no credit from all that I've heard about him." Sir Gilbert Carluke had been a gambler and a heavy drinker and a womanizer who had made his wife very unhappy, neglecting her and their son to spend much of his time on the Continent with some dubious friends. After an evening's drinking on a friend's yacht in Monte Carlo harbour, he had slipped and fallen into the sea and drowned some eight years before.

"Oh, he was never as wild as I'm reputed to be," Edward said smoothly.

"I shouldn't think anyone could be," Sylvie agreed, quite matter-of-fact.

His smile deepened. "I'm not as black as I'm painted. But you seem to know a lot about me and mine. Why is it that I know next to nothing about you?"

"Perhaps because my way of life

doesn't usually make headlines in all the newspapers, do you think?" she suggested with a disarming air of innocence.

He was delighted. He reached for the damp towel, lying close to his hand, crumpled it into a ball and threw it at her. Sylvie caught it, smiling.

He surveyed her for a moment, an appreciative glint in his eyes. Then he said lightly: "I'm afraid I didn't give you a very warm welcome yesterday. I didn't know I was going to like you so much."

There was a disturbing warmth behind the words. "Oh, I knew at once that I wasn't going to like you," she returned promptly.

His eyes narrowed. He wasn't quite sure if she was still teasing or in earnest. He wasn't quite sure about Sylvie Waring at all, he realized. Was she really as sweetly innocent and as disarmingly candid as she seemed? Or was she a very clever young woman? However it was, he did like her . . .

Sylvie reached for her sundress and towel and books. The sun was climbing high in the sky and she realized that they must have been romping like a couple of children for some time. "It must be time to get ready if we are to lunch with your friends."

"I'm looking forward to eating something, I must say," Edward declared. "I missed my breakfast to join you."

She was not flattered. "That was foolish — and I expect Miss Craig is wondering where you are," she said coolly. "If she does become an enemy I shall know that I have you to thank for it!"

Edward rose to his feet, tall, very bronzed and muscular, a very attractive man. "Miss Craig doesn't own me," he said shortly.

They walked back to the house together, the sun hot on their backs . . . and Diantha watched them from the terrace where she sat, leafing idly through a magazine.

She had only just come down from her room and she looked cool and lovely in a floral silk frock that was up-to-the-minute fashion. Hair, face and polished nails were as immaculate as careful and very skilled attention could make them. She was very beautiful. The look in her eyes was just a little ugly as they rested on the slight girl who walked with Edward, damp hair tousled and face flushed and eyes suspiciously bright. Diantha suspected that he had been making light love to the girl and she was very, very angry.

But she smiled and tossed aside her magazine as they mounted the stone steps to join her on the terrace. "Swimming! How very energetic," she drawled lightly. "I had no idea that you could be so active so early in the day, darling." The words held the faintest of mocking barbs.

Edward grinned and bent to kiss her, much too used to exciting jealousy in women to attach importance to it.

Sylvie, aware of a swift dislike of the

intimacy implied in that kiss, turned away and left them together. She knew that Diantha Craig looked after her and she felt very young, very gauche and very conscious of her untidy hair and naked face and the damp swimsuit that emphasized every line of her body. Without seeing the woman's expression, she knew that she was suspected of casting out lures to the sensual Edward and she was highly indignant.

Lunch with the Bryces turned into a party. Edward had taken advantage of a friendship that went back to boyhood to invite himself and Diantha. He had noticed that Leo was rather taken with the appealing Sylvie and it did not suit him to allow his friend a clear field. For one thing, he liked her, too. For another, he was inclined to use her to his own ends. Diantha was beginning to regard them as a couple and so did some of their friends. He had no intention of marrying the beautiful novelist. He did not particularly wish to marry at all. But if it was forced on

70

him then he would look for someone who readily adapted to his ideal of all that a wife should be — someone like the unspoiled Sylvie Waring, for instance . . .

Rylands was very old, a Tudor-built house set back from the road and separated from it by a large pond that was home to a variety of ducks. The house looked a little tumbledown with its ancient roof but its walls were stout and the interior with its heavy timbers and low ceilings and small leaded windows was very charming. Sylvie looked about her with delight. Leo, noticing, asked her if she was interested in old houses and their history and took her off to read the rhyme that was carved into the massive wooden surround of the fireplace in the hall.

"'*Yet Leo lives Ryelans thrives When Leo crumbles Ryelans tumbles . . .* '" she quoted, a little wonderingly. She turned to him, eyes bright. "What does it mean?"

"Rylands was built for a man named

Hubert Leo and his descendants lived here for many years, apparently. But eventually the name died out and the house stood empty and fell into disrepair although the land was farmed by neighbours who leased it. My grandfather was the son of a prosperous manufacturer who wanted to farm and he fell in love with Rylands and bought it. His name was Leonard and he regarded it as a good omen when he read that rhyme. My mother was born here and christened Leonie. She died soon after Lucinda was born and our father returned to his native New Zealand, leaving us to be brought up by my grandmother. So Rylands has been my home for as long as I can remember."

"And you are really named Leonard?"

"No. Just Leo. My mother knew I would inherit with time and she wanted to keep on the right side of the old legend. Now Rylands is mine and it hasn't tumbled yet, I'm glad to say."

"I think that's fascinating!" Sylvie

declared warmly. "I suppose you'll follow tradition and name your son Leo, too?"

"I've yet to find myself a wife," he pointed out, smiling.

"Well, that shouldn't be difficult . . . oh, I'm sorry!" She was blushing and confused as she realized where her unruly tongue had led her.

Leo laughed. "You're very kind. But, like Edward, I'm not in any hurry to be married."

"Taking my name in vain?" Edward had strolled in search of them and stood, unnoticed, watching them from the far end of the hall. Now he came forward, drawling the words.

"Sylvie thinks I should secure the future of Rylands by marrying and bringing another Leo into the world," he explained lightly. "I was just saying that, like you, I've been a bachelor so long that I'm not sure that marriage will suit me!"

"Oh, it will suit me well enough when the time comes," Edward said carelessly. "And that may be sooner than most people expect." He laughed. "I shall confound all my critics by making some lucky woman an excellent husband!"

"Do you have some lucky woman in mind?" Leo's tone was light, amused, but his eyes were very intent on Edward's handsome face.

Edward laid one long finger along the side of his nose in an age-old gesture of secrecy. "Someone not a million miles from here," he said mischievously, his dark eyes twinkling. "*Entre nous* . . ."

Sylvie knew that he referred to her and she knew that he was far from serious. It was rapidly becoming a little game, she thought, half-amused, half-irritated.

But Leo's eyes darkened and the hand that rested on the mantel suddenly clenched in betrayal. For he thought that his friend spoke of Diantha and he immediately felt that, legend or no legend, he must leave Rylands if the woman he loved came to the neighbouring Chase Hall as Edward's wife.

"I shall believe it when I see a wedding ring on her finger," he forced himself to say, as lightly as he could.

Edward laughed, unaware of his friend's torment of heart and mind. He had never supposed that Diantha and Leo were anything but friends. They seemed fond of each other but there had never been any hint of a greater intimacy in their relationship. But, being the man that he was, it would probably not have deflected him when he first saw and wanted the beautiful Diantha Craig if he had known that Leo loved and hoped to marry her. In his book, all was fair in love and war!

Lucinda created a welcome diversion by calling them in to eat. She was a very pretty girl, cast much in Diantha's mould with her love of clothes and jewels and expensive living, but she was more to Sylvie's liking. Partly because they were closer in age but also because Lucinda had no reason to resent her presence and she welcomed a new friend with all the enthusiasm of one who liked novelty.

Sylvie noticed that Edward's attitude to the pretty Lucinda bordered on the brotherly and she was honest enough to admit that the fact coloured her view of the girl to some extent. It was quite absurd but she knew that her intense dislike of Diantha Craig was fired by a reluctant attraction for the man who was obviously the woman's lover.

She was far from being in love with Edward Carluke. She was much too level-headed for that, she told herself confidently. But she did like him — when she was not disliking and despising him for his outrageous behaviour! And it was impossible to deny that her senses swam at his merest touch — although she would die rather than let him know it!

# 4

SHE had an excellent seat. Born to the saddle, Edward approved, spurring his own mount to a canter in pursuit. Sylvie glanced over her shoulder, laughing, betraying a youthful delight in her skilful management of the glossy chestnut mare. The horse was a little restive and she had chosen to allow her to stretch her legs in a fast canter across the fields, leaving the others to follow at a more leisurely pace.

Her long hair streamed in the wind that horse and rider created and as she reined and turned the mare to meet him, it whipped about her laughing face. He had not thought her lovely until that moment. Pretty, yes . . . quite appealing, a little intriguing. His interest quickened abruptly.

He reined his own horse beside her and smiled, admiring and approving.

"You have the edge on Diantha and you know it," he said softly, humorously, teasing her gently.

Diantha rode because it was a necessary accomplishment in her social circle. But she was not really at home on a horse. Knowing it, Leo had mounted her on the sweet-mouthed mare he had intended for Sylvie, the gentlest and easiest of his horses. His own favourite, the chestnut high-stepper, had seemed a good choice for the girl he had seen flying across the fields on one of Edward's horses, proving her competence as a rider. He was mounted on a big black stallion, the latest addition to his stables, while Lucinda rode her own grey mare. Edward had opted to ride a rather bad-tempered horse that he had sold to Leo, knowing that his friend would sweeten his temperament as he could not.

Sylvie glanced at the rather set expression on Diantha's lovely face. She looked at Edward, a little dismayed. "I didn't intend . . . "

" . . . To parade your superior horsemanship?" he finished for her, lightly. "You ride superbly, you know."

"That will commend me to your friend," she said dryly.

"Do you care?"

She shrugged. He noticed the curve of her small, enticing breasts beneath the bright yellow jumper she was wearing with her jodhpurs. Desire stirred. Sylvie, woman-like, was aware of that flickering glance and the swift glint in his dark eyes and a little colour stole into her face.

She spurred the mare and trotted across the field to join the others, wondering if Edward Carluke deliberately and mischievously sought to annoy Diantha by making her the doubtful object of his attentions — and wished he would not. He kept forcing himself on her notice when she would be quite happy to ignore him as much as possible, she thought crossly.

"She has had her head for a few

minutes and now she will behave," she declared lightly, reaching Leo's side.

"She needed to stretch her legs," he agreed. He smiled at Sylvie with warm liking. "What do you think of her?" His tone conveyed his conviction that she knew enough about horses to give a reliable opinion.

Sylvie patted the mare's glossy, arched neck. "A nice girl," she approved warmly. "Youthful high spirits but amenable to a firm hand on the rein. I should be happy to have one like her in the stables at home!"

Diantha felt that far too much attention was being paid to the girl by Edward who pursued almost anything in skirts and by Leo who was amazingly responsive to a quite blatant bid for his interest. Sylvie Waring was becoming more confident by the minute — and more of a threat, she thought irritably.

"No doubt you ride a great deal," she said sweetly, managing to make it seem a most unfeminine pursuit. "I suppose there isn't much else to do in your part of the world. I'm afraid I prefer people to horses. The conversation is so much more stimulating. Leo darling, I'm hot and thirsty," she added, looking as cool and lovely as when they set out. "Will you forgive me if I turn back?"

"But we'll ride with you," he said promptly, quite forgetting that the object of the exercise had been to show Sylvie over as many of his acres as possible. "Does anyone want to go on? It really is too hot for comfort and I think we could all use a long, cool drink."

There was general agreement and the horses were turned and headed for home at a leisurely pace that was almost ambling. Diantha sat her horse like a beautiful queen with a courtier on either side. Sylvie and Lucinda brought up the rear.

"I wonder if Edward means to marry her," Lucinda said idly, confident that there was sufficient distance between them for her words to reach Sylvie's ears only.

"I've no idea." Sylvie's tone was cool, discouraging. She had no desire to discuss Edward Carluke's probable intentions.

"She's lasted longer than most." Lucinda was deaf to the careful indifference of the response. "He's usually so fickle that one can't help wondering if he's serious this time. She's very lovely, don't you think?"

"Very."

"And clever! I admire her tremendously. I think everyone must. I wonder if she makes a great deal of money from her books? Edward is dreadfully in debt, you know," Lucinda swept on in her thoughtless fashion. "He needs to marry for money if he is to keep the Hall, Leo says. Perhaps Diantha is rich enough to tempt him."

Sylvie did not answer. She found that her heart was beating very fast, angrily. She discovered that she did not like the thought that Edward might marry Diantha Craig. She visualized him smiling into those beautiful eyes, kissing that beautiful mouth, drawing that beautiful body into his arms — and a fierce dislike of going further with those thoughts caused her to jerk so violently at the rein that the mare reared in alarm and threw her off.

Lucinda's cry caused the others to glance back. Amused satisfaction leaped to Diantha's eyes. Leo looked concerned. Edward reacted more swiftly than either of them, bringing his horse round on the instant and cantering back to where Sylvie lay, not hurt but a little shaken and a good deal mortified.

He swung himself from the saddle and bent over her. A little anxiety in the dark eyes gave way to amusement as he realized that she was unhurt. "How hath the mighty fallen," he murmured mockingly, gathering her into his arms and lifting her up with ease. She was briefly crushed against his powerful chest and she fancied that his lips brushed her forehead. Then she was on her feet, steadied by his hand at her elbow. "All right . . . ?"

"Quite," she said proudly, furious with herself. She did not need to glance in Diantha Craig's direction to know how much that woman must be enjoying her discomfiture.

Leo reached them in that moment. "My dear girl — what happened!" He leaped to the ground. "Are you hurt?"

"Only my pride," she said with a rueful smile. "It was entirely my fault. I brought Firefly up short for no reason and she naturally took exception to it." She moved gingerly towards the mare who stood quietly, head lowered to graze, her bridle firmly held by Lucinda.

"You *are* hurt!" Leo exclaimed, concerned.

"One or two bruises, perhaps. Nothing worse than that." She smiled at him very warmly, touched by his anxiety.

A little frown leaped to Edward's dark eyes. He was beginning to regard Leo as a serious rival — and it irked him that Sylvie responded so warmly to his friend. He re-mounted and rode off to join Diantha.

Humiliated by the incident, Sylvie held her head very high. Leo stayed close, telling her about his many tumbles through the years. She knew that he meant to put her at her ease and warmed to him. At the same time, it was galling that he obviously did not trust her not to be unseated again when she had been put on a horse at the tender age of three and taken to riding like a duck to water! It would not have mattered so much if Diantha Craig had not witnessed her humiliation . . . or if Edward had not seemed so unconcerned, she thought, forgetting how swiftly he had come to her aid.

He rode ahead with Diantha, their horses very close together. Sylvie noted how often the dark head was bent to the bright auburn one. They made a very handsome couple, she admitted reluctantly. And the novelist was very much of his world. Sylvie thought it very likely that the woman was in love with Edward. Could he be in love with her when he seemed so ready to flirt with his mother's guest? Or was that mere expediency? Deeply in debt, desperate to keep his home, perhaps he was toying with the idea of marriage to a girl he did not really know.

A little bleakly, Sylvie wished that she was not the daughter of a very wealthy man. Then she might not have to wonder if Edward Carluke liked her or the thought of her father's money.

It did not really matter, of course. For if he did ask her to marry him, she would refuse. She wanted to love the man she married. She wanted to be very sure of her future happiness when she took the most important step in her life. She wanted to be loved. Edward Carluke could not fulfil any of those requirements, obviously.

They stayed to tea at Rylands, lazing in the warm sunshine. Knowing that Leo had referred to riding, Diantha had wisely brought jodphurs with her and she changed back into her floral silk frock as soon as they returned from the stables. Complete with fashionably large sunglasses, she looked coolly elegant and very self-possessed. Sylvie sweltered in jumper and jodhpurs. As unobtrusively as possible, she edged her chair into a little shade and thought how much she might have enjoyed the afternoon if she could have been alone with the pleasant and friendly Bryces. As it was, Diantha Craig contrived to make her feel very much the outsider with her constant references to past events and mutual friends.

She found Edward by her side with the ice bucket. "Let me refresh your drink," he said lightly.

"Thank you." Sylvie was not grateful to him for drawing attention to her discomfort.

He stood over her with a large lump of ice held in the tongs, a little mischief in his dark eyes. "You won't allow me to warm you up," he murmured softly, eyes dancing. "Perhaps I may cool you down."

She smiled without warmth.

Diantha could not hear what he said. But the laughter in his expression was unmistakable. "Don't tease the poor child, darling," she called gently. "What a boy you are!" The affectionate indulgence in that light reproach was very marked, hinting at the closeness of their relationship.

Sylvie saw the flicker of a frown cross his handsome face. Then he dropped the piece of ice into her glass of lemonade and returned the bucket to its place on the trolley. He did not return to his seat by Diantha . . . and that served her jolly well right, thought Sylvie with a very human satisfaction. He strolled down to the edge of the duck pond and began to feed the birds with a couple of sandwiches he had taken from a plate in passing. She watched him while Diantha chatted lightly to Leo and Lucinda as though she did not know that he was annoyed and she was snubbed.

Sylvie was surprised that such a clever woman could be so foolish. Anyone could see with half an eye that Edward Carluke was a proud and private man who would object to his intimate relationship with a woman being aired in public. The offence lay not in the meaningless words but the way in which they had been uttered. Perhaps Diantha Craig was not so sure of him as she seemed. Or perhaps she had only wanted to warn her off, Sylvie thought shrewdly. Whether he was only flirting because he could not help it or trying to irritate Diantha for reasons of his own, he was paying her a certain amount of attention. Not enough to make her feel that she attracted him particularly but certainly enough to shake another woman's confidence.

Watching as the ducks scudded hastily across the pond and snatched greedily at the pieces of bread that he threw to them, Sylvie felt drawn to Edward Carluke by an odd little tug at her emotions. She knew that he was spoiled and arrogant and unreliable, a shocking rake that no woman should trust with her heart or her happiness. But he *was* attractive, she thought, a little wistfully. It would be dangerously easy to respond to the charm in his smile, his warm personality, his gift for making a woman feel that she was the only one in his world, however briefly. There were moments when she liked him very well for all the moments when she did not like him at all . . .

It seemed that he had forgiven Diantha for he swept her off to a nightclub in the nearby town to dine and dance that evening. Sylvie was left to spend the evening with Lady Carluke and did so quite happily, refusing to remember how beautiful Diantha had looked in the cloud of misty grey tulle with diamonds sparkling against her breast and about her throat and in her ears. They played backgammon after dinner and Sylvie, a newcomer to the game, was delighted to win.

"Good heavens! I'm in debt to the tune of forty-two thousand," Lady Carluke exclaimed in mock dismay.

"I lost sixty thousand to you the other evening. So you still have something in credit," Sylvie reminded her, eyes dancing.

"Thank goodness we aren't playing for real! I'm not a gambler, I'm afraid. Nor is Edward, I'm glad to say. At least, not in the way that his father was! Gilbert would wager a thousand pounds on which of two birds on the lawn would fly away first, my dear! Edward has rather more respect for money but I expect that's because there isn't very much of it since his father died," she sighed. "This place must be a great burden to him but I know he won't part with it unless it's forced on him . . . and that may happen, of course. But I mustn't weary you with our problems, child," she added, smiling, patting Sylvie's hand. She felt a little glow of affection for the girl, so refreshingly unaffected, so delightful in her ready enjoyment of even the smallest pleasure, so pretty with those enormous grey eyes fixed on one's face with a little concern in their depths.

"This is your home," Sylvie said slowly. "How could you bear to leave it after so many years? It's so beautiful, too."

"It is beautiful and I would miss it, of course," she agreed. "But I've always planned to move to the Dower House when Edward marries, you know. It's a charming house and I shall be very happy there. Young couples don't want an elderly invalid under their feet and invading their privacy."

"But if Edward has to sell . . . "

Lady Carluke looked just a little self-conscious. "Yes . . . well — that depends so much on circumstances, you know."

"On whether or not he finds himself a rich wife?" Sylvie suggested, a little dryly.

"Well . . . yes," Lady Carluke said, flustered.

"And I suppose it doesn't matter very much whether or not he loves her?" she said quietly.

Lady Carluke was silent for a moment. Then she took Sylvie's hand and said gently: "Naturally, one hopes . . . Edward's happiness means a great deal to me. You're very young and a little romantic and I daresay it seems quite dreadful to you. But I assure you that it is just as easy to love someone with money as without it . . . particularly if she is young and pretty and sweet-natured."

It was impossible for Sylvie to mistake the meaning behind the words. She stiffened. Then, carefully, not wishing to offend someone who had been kind and affectionate towards her for whatever motive, she said: "I could never marry Edward. I don't dislike him but we come from very different worlds. He wouldn't be happy with me — and I would always know that he married Hugh Waring's daughter."

Lady Carluke sighed. "You're a

perceptive child. I won't deny that I had hopes. I'm very fond of you, Sylvie. I think you could make my son very happy. But I do understand your feelings . . . of course I do! Why, you don't suppose that Gilbert Carluke married me for love, do you? He had gambled away a fortune and needed to replace it. I loved him and coaxed my father into accepting the match. But I always knew how Gilbert felt about me. He wasn't the kind of man to pretend."

"Nor is Edward, I imagine," Sylvie said firmly.

"He is very like his father in some ways," Lady Carluke agreed reluctantly. She drew Sylvie towards her and kissed the soft cheek. "Now, don't run away with the idea that I invited you solely to marry you off to my son! I was very fond of your dear mother and I've wanted to know you for a very long time. But your father would never allow me to invite you here until now. I'm so glad that he changed his mind."

"I think he suddenly realized that I'd grown up when he wasn't looking," Sylvie said lightly. "He doesn't want to lose me but I think he feels that I ought to have the same opportunities as other girls to meet eligible young men. But I'm surprised that he thought Edward might be a suitable husband for me. He has a shocking reputation, you know."

And one of the oldest and most honourable of names, and his title gives him a social standing that Hugh Waring might well want for his daughter, Lady Carluke thought shrewdly. She smiled on Sylvic with warmth. "I don't believe more than a third of the things that people say about him — and I hope you won't either! He was always a mischievous boy and I think he delights in giving the gossips something to talk about. My dear, isn't it time for that programme we were going to watch?"

The television was switched on and they watched a documentary on wild life followed by the late news. Then Lady Carluke said goodnight and went up to her room, leaving Sylvie to watch a film. She found that she did not like it and she curled up on the sofa with a book. She was reluctant to go tamely to bed. She did not mean to wait up until Edward and Diantha returned, of course. They would obviously be very late for they lived in a world that liked to turn night into day.

The book bored her. She put it aside and wandered out to the terrace. But the moon was concealed by dark clouds and there was a chill in the air and the shadows seemed a little eerie. She returned to the drawing-room and went to the piano. Sitting down, she began to play, her fingers straying idly across the keys at first, her thoughts busy. But soon she was lost in the pleasure of playing. She had a nice touch, a real feeling for music, and it had always been one of her comforts. For all her quiet way of life, she had never been lonely. She had too many interests for the days to hang heavily on her hands. It was only because she was a stranger at Chase Hall that she knew a melancholy that might almost be loneliness.

The haunting strains of a Chopin nocturne greeted Edward as he entered the room. He paused, listened . . . and quietly closed the door. She did not seem to be aware of him, a slight, intent figure at the piano, her head bent over the keyboard. She could play very well, he thought, surprised by the range of her accomplishments. Most of the girls that he knew seemed only able to be beautiful. Sylvie combined her prettiness with a variety of talents and a good deal of intelligence.

He sat down in a comfortable wing chair and Sylvie continued to play, unconscious of his presence. Edward relaxed. Diantha had gone to her room, a trifle annoyed that he had refused to be pinned down when she hinted at the future of their relationship. He fancied that she was already rattled by his interest in Sylvie Waring. She was not being very clever and that was not like the lovely Diantha Craig, he thought dryly.

Rather ruffled from that civilized clash with Diantha, he was tempted to think seriously about a future that did not include her at all. His dark eyes were very intent as he studied Sylvie, knowing that he was interested, even attracted. She was appealing. She had character and spirit. His mother liked and approved the girl. He could do very much worse than marry her, he felt. He had loved a dozen women and proved to his own satisfaction that love did not last. He did not expect to love the woman he eventually married and he would certainly not ask that she loved him. Liking, a certain amount of physical attraction, mutual interests, and a sensible determination to make the marriage work was all that was necessary. Sylvie seemed to have all the right qualifications . . .

Sylvie suddenly knew that odd sensation of hair rising on the back of her neck. Her hands fell from the keyboard and she swung round, her heart quickening. She was startled to find that she was no longer alone in the room . . . and disconcerted to find his dark eyes upon her, intently serious.

Then he smiled.

"How long have you been there?" she demanded, feeling at a disadvantage.

"Only a few minutes. I've been enjoying the music and wondering what other talents you have that I've yet to discover."

Sylvie crossed the room to sit on the sofa. "None," she said firmly, suspecting a hidden meaning behind seemingly innocent words.

He raised an eyebrow. "I don't believe you."

"Where's Diantha?"

"Gone to bed." His smile deepened. "I wouldn't ask her to marry me and she isn't very pleased with me at the moment."

Sylvie frowned. "I don't think you should tell me such things," she said disapprovingly.

"I did warn you that I'm not a gentleman," he said lightly, his eyes twinkling.

"I can't imagine why any woman would want to marry you," Sylvie said in a conversational tone. "You have nothing to recommend you but a handsome face."

Amused, Edward returned: "You are forgetting the title, Sylvie. It's a great attraction."

"But you're only a baronet," she pointed out.

"You would aim higher, I daresay?"

"I don't mean to marry at all," she said firmly.

He laughed softly. "If you are in that mood then I won't even try to tempt you!"

She looked at him quickly, alarm in her heart. "I hope you will never try." She spoke quietly but with force.

Edward sobered. He leaned forward to look into her troubled face. "My Mama wishes me to marry you. Is the idea so very distasteful to you, Sylvie?"

She wished he would not take her name and make of it an endearment. How could there be so much tenderness in a man's voice when she meant nothing to him? How was it possible to be drawn by the thought of marrying a man she did not love, who did not love her?

"Surely it must be distasteful to you, too!" she exclaimed.

He looked at her with a smile in his dark eyes. "No. But you have so much more to recommend you than a pretty face, you know."

He was not thinking of her father's money in that moment. It seemed to Sylvie that he could not be thinking of anything else.

"Then I ought to be able to do very much better for myself when it comes to finding a husband, don't you think?" she said sweetly, fuming. "An impoverished Earl, perhaps!"

"You misunderstand . . . " he began.

"I understand perfectly well," she told him coldly, rising, pride in every inch of that small figure. "Goodnight, Edward."

Edward swore as the door closed behind her. He had not been leading up to a proposal of marriage, as it happened. But if he had then his stupid handling of a sensitive girl would certainly have earned him a much-deserved refusal!

# 5

"**D**O you play tennis as well as you play the piano, I wonder?"

Edward smiled at her across the breakfast table. It was the nearest he would get to an apology, she suspected . . . and wished she did not find it so easy to forgive him when she met those smiling dark eyes, so warm, so very attractive.

"That's a loaded question," she returned lightly. "A yes or a no will earn me the label of conceit."

His smile deepened with swift appreciation of her quick intellect. "I will rephrase it. Do you play tennis?"

"As long as you are not expecting Wimbledon standards."

"Which probably means that you play very much better than I do," he said dryly. "Will you give me a game?"

Sylvie hesitated. "Doesn't Diantha play?"

"Diantha doesn't take kindly to most forms of exercise. She has brought the proofs of her new book for checking and means to spend the morning quietly on the terrace."

"I did bring my tennis things with me in the hope of getting a game," Sylvie admitted.

"Good girl!" He smiled his approval. It was infuriating that she should feel that she was forgiven when *he* had offended! She rose from the table. "I'll go and change."

He was practising his service on the tennis court when she joined him, a trim figure in the short white tennis frock, her pale hair banded neatly about her head.

"My God! You're a professional!" he declared teasingly. "I don't stand a chance!"

Sylvie smiled, expecting that she would need to be on her mettle. Her father was an exceptionally good player who had been seeded at Wimbledon in his youth and he had taught her well. For all her slight build, she had a strong arm. But Edward was cunning and caught her out with the unexpected shot . . . and she felt that it was a tribute to her game that he did not make the smallest allowance for her sex.

Edward won — but only after a very good game which proved that they were evenly matched. They came off the court, the very best of friends, his arm about her shoulders, both slightly breathless and elated.

Sylvie looked up at him, laughing. "That was fun!"

"You're too good for me," he told her warmly. "That last point was sheer fluke. I can't remember when I've enjoyed a game so much, you know." He hugged her to him impulsively. "I think I'm afraid of you, Sylvie," he added lightly. "You're so unexpected!"

Meeting the laughter in his eyes, mingled with admiration and liking,

Sylvie felt her heart lurch. She felt very conscious of him as he held her, smiling down at her, suddenly a very real threat to her peace of mind. "I think I'm afraid of you," she returned as lightly as she could. "You're so predictable!"

His arm tightened. "Am I?" He drew her against him. "So you know that I'm about to kiss you — the winner's trophy!"

She knew she should pull out of those enfolding arms. But the look in his dark eyes held her like a spell of enchantment. Her body was melting in his embrace and his physical magnetism was playing havoc with all her proud resolutions. She wanted him to kiss her and she was in no mood to resist . . .

His lips teased her soft, sweetly-scented hair, her temple, the tempting curve of her smooth cheek. Manlike, he was delighting in the soft warmth of her body against his own. He was in no hurry to end the embrace and he knew that nine-tenths of the pleasure in any kiss was in its anticipation.

His mouth hovered at the corner of her own and Sylvie was drowning in the sweet flood of desire triggered by his nearness. Her arms stole about his neck in unconscious response and her body arched, betraying the yearning that he evoked.

Unnoticed by either of them, Diantha stood by the hedge that bordered the tennis court, watching them with anger in her eyes. She wondered why she did not simply walk out of Edward's life and be done with him. He was incapable of caring deeply for any woman, she thought bitterly. But she was captivated by his looks, his charm, his physical attractions — and anyone who loved Edward Carluke had to accept that it was quite impossible for him to be faithful. He was an opportunist who could not resist a pretty face. But Sylvie Waring was more of a threat than most, Diantha thought grimly. For she was the daughter of a man who could solve all Edward's financial problems at a stroke — and that must be a very tempting carrot to lure a man into marriage.

She moved forward, saying lightly and with seeming unconcern: "Claim your kiss, Edward. You certainly deserve it. I've never seen you play so well!"

They broke apart instantly.

Edward was furious but only the narrowing of his dark eyes betrayed his fierce disappointment. She had been so near to giving him those sweet lips of her own volition.

He smiled as he turned to Diantha and said smoothly: "I had to play well. Sylvie is a champion!"

"Really?" Diantha simulated interest. "The local tennis club?"

"I'm not a champion. That's just Edward's nonsense," Sylvie said shortly, mortified at having been caught in his arms by the woman who undoubtedly had a prior claim on him. She bent down to retrieve the racket that had slipped from her hand to the grass, wishing that the ground would open and swallow her up.

It had seemed that she stood in his arms for an eternity. Perhaps it had been only a moment or two in reality. But Diantha must have seen that eager, almost shameful response and probably suspected her of throwing herself at Edward's head. She had never been so embarrassed. She felt that she was aflame from head to toe.

They walked back to the house. Sylvie was silent, all her pleasure in the day suddenly destroyed. Edward was entirely at his ease, talking lightly about the proofs for the new book that was apparently due to be published in the autumn.

Sylvie realized the enormous gulf between herself and someone like Diantha Craig, so clever, so successful, so famous. She might be able to ride, play the piano, sketch a little, play tennis rather well. But she could not compete with Diantha who belonged to his world.

There was no question of competing,

of course. The very fact that Edward talked so frankly to her about his mother's wishes meant that he had not the slightest idea of asking her to marry him, she knew. She did not wish to marry him. His foolish impact on her emotions would be forgotten as soon as she returned to Cornwall. She had been invited to stay for a few weeks. It would be too pointed if she left after only a few days — and she certainly did not mean to give Diantha Craig the satisfaction of supposing that she had driven her away!

She showered and wrapped a thick towel about herself and was hesitating over the array of summer frocks in her wardrobe when there was a tap at the door of the adjoining sitting-room.

Edward put his head around the door. "May I come in?" He entered and closed the door behind him.

"No!" Sylvie said vehemently from the threshold of the bedroom, abruptly aware that she was clad only in a towel that revealed much of her long, slender legs and bared her sloping shoulders.

He looked at her with mischievous appreciation. "Very nice," he approved.

She backed into the bedroom hastily. "What do you want?"

"I came for my kiss," he said, teasing her gently. "I won fair and square and I don't see why I should be cheated out of my trophy."

She closed the door and set her back against it. "Please go away, Edward!"

He laughed. "Don't you trust me?"

"Not in the least!"

"I came to say that Diantha and I are going to the Country Club for lunch and a game of golf," he told her lightly, reassuring her. "Do you care to come with us? Leo might make it a foursome."

"I don't play golf." Sylvie scrambled into underthings and reached for the first dress that came to hand ... a heavy cream linen with square neckline and pleated skirt.

"You disappoint me! Diantha plays extremely well," he told her, a little mockingly. He hesitated. "Come, anyway . . . "

"And play gooseberry? No, thanks!" She slipped her slender feet into matching shoes and, feeling rather more able to cope with him now that she was dressed, opened the door to the sitting-room.

Edward smiled at her. "I think I prefer the towel," he said, his dark eyes dancing with mischief.

"I'm not interested in your preferences." A little colour crept into her small face.

"Hoity-toity!"

She smiled reluctantly. "I wish you wouldn't keep Diantha waiting. I am not her favourite person just now and you aren't improving matters."

"I rather think you're mine," he said softly.

Sylvie refused to be flattered. She had to be very firm with the heart that threatened to leap with delight at words he could not possibly mean.

She was silent.

Edward studied the flushed face, very lovely to him, and noticed how reluctant she was to meet his eyes. Her shyness, her obvious embarrassment, her inexperience of even the mildest flirtation, touched him unexpectedly. She was delightful, really an enchanting girl, much more appealing in that moment than all the Dianthas.

He stretched out a hand to touch the soft, glowing cheek in an involuntary caress. She stood still, unresponsive.

Edward disliked the swift suspicion that she rebuffed him out of indifference rather than a feminine desire to quicken his interest. It seemed that it was going to take longer than he had anticipated to break through her reserve. She was tantalizing in the occasional hint of a response that would delight any man . . . but he sensed that it was instinctive rather than the usual feminine tactics. All the more desirable for that very reason, he thought, refusing to be rebuffed.

He turned away with a careless ease

of manner. "I'm sorry you won't join us. Another time, perhaps?"

Sylvie smiled politely but made no other response and he went from the room. In her mind's eye, she followed him as he ran lithely down the broad staircase to join the waiting Diantha, dismissing her almost before the door had closed. He could only have invited her out of a well-bred courtesy towards his mother's guest, she realized. They could not truly wish for the company of an inconvenient third.

In her mind's eye, she saw them leave the house together, walk to his waiting car, his arm about the slim waist and his smile caressing the loving Diantha with intimate warmth.

Sylvie shrugged off the teasing and oddly disturbing images. As if it mattered to her that they were lovers. *She* did not want Edward Carluke, she averred stoutly.

It seemed a very long afternoon. Perhaps it was too hot but she had very little appetite for the delicious lunch that was served to Lady Carluke and herself. Afterwards, she tried to read, to write a letter to her father, to be interested in the women's programmes on the radio that her companion obviously enjoyed while occupying her skilful hands with her tapestry. She picked up her sketchbook and put it down again. She wandered about the garden and amused herself with removing the dead heads from the rose bushes. She walked down to the lake and back again with Hero trotting at her side like the well-behaved matron that she was.

Lady Carluke looked at the rather wistful figure with a faint frown. The girl did not seem to know what to do with herself. She suspected that Edward had unsettled her for she had seemed happy enough until his return. He was such an attractive man and he had the very dangerous charm of the Carlukes. She sighed, remembering that she had fallen headlong in love at first sight with his father. Well, she had wanted to marry him and she had got her way — and little good it had done her! Gilbert had been handsome but wayward and unscrupulous and quite heartless. He had broken more hearts than her own. Edward was very like him but not, she hoped, quite heartless or beyond redemption. He was very spoiled, of course. Much too attractive for his own good, unfortunately — and the women seemed unable to refuse him anything. She must keep a careful eye on Sylvie. She was little more than a child and quite inexperienced . . . just at the age to tumble helplessly into love and Edward was quite selfish enough to encourage her for his own ends!

They returned in time for tea. Diantha had holed in one and was very animated, very pleased with herself. Over tea, she enjoyed describing the game minutely while a patient Lady Carluke listened . . . and Edward, bored with the subject by this time, sank into the sofa by Sylvie's side. He reached for the book she was reading.

"Not one of Diantha's, I see," he said lightly, glancing at the title and then at one or two of the pages. "Don't you read romance?"

"Not very often."

He glanced at her. "I rather thought you were a romantic, you know. I expect you *are* at heart like every woman."

"No, I'm not. I'm a very practical person with my feet firmly on the ground." She reached to retrieve her book.

"What have you been doing with yourself this afternoon? Amusing my mama?" He smiled at her.

"I'm very happy in her company," she told him firmly, determined that he should not suspect how bored and oddly lost she had been without him.

"I expect you miss your mother," he said gently, unexpectedly.

The note of sympathy caused tears to prick her eyes. She blinked. "Yes, I do."

"Well, I'm happy to share my mama

117

with you," he told her, pressing her hand briefly in understanding. "You are just the sort of daughter she has always wanted, you know. Good-natured, well-behaved and really very sweet."

Sylvie looked at him suspiciously, believing that he was laughing at her. "I don't trust your compliments."

He met her eyes steadily. "For once, I am sincere. I do think you're sweet."

She rose and went to help Lady Carluke with dispensing tea and sandwiches and cake. *Sweet*, she thought bitterly, far from pleased. Anyone could be sweet! Diantha Craig was most unlikely to be described so patronizingly — and Diantha Craig was apparently the kind of woman he liked to have about him. Sylvie did not want him to regard her as *sweet*!

Edward was intrigued by that rather stormy light in the expressive grey eyes. He wondered how he had managed to annoy her. It had been unintentional. She was so enchantingly young that he liked to tease her. But he had felt so grateful to her for bringing a new interest and a new purpose to his mother's life that he had been entirely in earnest. He liked her very, very much. But sometimes she was as prickly as a hedgehog . . . the sensitivity of extreme youth, he thought indulgently.

Briefly alone with his mother that evening, he spoke of her with a warmth that did not escape her perceptive notice.

"She's a nice child," he said. "I'm afraid you will miss her when she leaves the Hall. How long does she mean to stay?"

"Oh, just a few weeks. Hugh Waring is in New York, I understand . . . deeply involved in some new financial venture. He was pleased to accept my invitation to have Sylvie here while he's away and I'm delighted to have her . . . dear Frances' daughter," she said with a soft, reminiscent sigh. "She *is* a nice child. I'm very fond of her."

He poured himself a drink. "You

will miss her," he repeated, thinking how much happier, how much more animated she seemed with the girl for company. He was often away or busy with estate affairs. He supposed his mother might be lonely but she had always rejected his suggestion of a paid companion.

Lady Carluke mused thoughtfully: "I wonder if he thought I might find her a husband? She seems to have met hardly any men. I thought Leo was very taken with her. Did you notice, Edward? He may be rather too old for her, of course . . ."

"He's all of a year older than me," Edward agreed, amused.

She swept on as though he had not spoken: " . . . but she seems to like him. Don't you think so?"

He frowned. It seemed to him that Sylvie did like Leo . . . rather more than she liked him, anyway. It was difficult to know just what she thought and felt where he was concerned, in fact. She was young but she could keep her own counsel very successfully.

"I think it's a mistake to try your hand at match making, Mama," he said lightly.

Lady Carluke ignored him. "I'm afraid Hugh Waring has kept her much too close," she mused. "The young need to try their wings before leaving the nest. Sylvie ought to meet the right kind of young men if she is not to make a foolish marriage."

"Then it was most unwise of you to invite her here," he drawled, eyes twinkling. "Fathers of marriageable daughters do not consider me to be the right kind of young man, you know."

"My dear Edward, I knew better than to expect that such a sweet and unaffected and thoroughly nice girl would appeal to you," she told him, rather dryly. "Besides, if you thought that I'd only invited her as a possible wife for you, you would do your utmost to push her into Leo's arms!"

He bent to kiss her cheek, his dark

eyes dancing. "I'm a sore trial to you, I'm afraid."

"You must marry one day — and you could do worse than take Sylvie Waring," she said, clinging to him for a moment. He was very dear and she did want his happiness and she did not believe that he would ever find it with a woman like Diantha Craig.

If only he could fall truly and deeply in love with a nice girl, she sighed. It might be the making of her sensual, selfish son!

"I would do anything to please you. But I doubt if the girl would have me," he said carelessly.

She looked into the laughing eyes. "She has a head on her shoulders," she said dryly. "I was afraid that she might fall for your good looks like too many girls of that age."

"I expect she prefers fair men — and Leo would make her a very good husband." His tone was indifferent.

"I believe you are right. I shall do what I can to encourage the affair,"

Lady Carluke announced with a little air of resolution that did not deceive her perceptive son for a moment.

He smiled down at her with very tender, very loving affection . . . and Sylvie, walking into the room at that moment, knew that her heart contracted with a foolish wish that he would look at her with that particular glow in his handsome face.

"What will you drink, Sylvie?" He crossed to the decanters. "Sherry, gin, vodka . . . ?"

At least, he was attentive, she thought. He was the perfect host . . . when others were present. It was only when they were alone that the little devil lurked in his dark eyes and he seemed to delight in discomfiting her. "Sherry, please."

"How pretty you look, my dear. Such a delightful dress." Lady Carluke's tone was as warm as her approving eyes.

"I remembered that you liked it when Colonel and Mrs Ingrams came to dinner." Sylvie took her drink and thanked Edward with a brief smile. She hoped he did not suppose that she had dressed for his benefit!

It was a pretty dress with its low, rounded neckline and puff sleeves, palest pink graduating to deepest rose in varying shades. She wore a simple row of very good pearls and matching pearl drops in her small ears. She had piled her hair high in a Grecian knot of curls, banded with a deep rose ribbon to match her dress. She wore a dusting of powder and a little lipstick. She looked refreshingly natural and very lovely, thought Edward, with an appreciation that for once did not border on the sensual.

He bent over her and murmured wickedly: "I wonder why I thought you were an orphan child when I first set eyes on you?"

Sylvie blushed, remembering that first meeting and her own confusion and instinctive resentment and dislike of him. "I'd been rambling in the copse with Hero and hadn't had time to change. You wouldn't expect me to wear good clothes to explore the woods," she said, a little defensively. "You weren't expected until much later in the day."

"How you must have hated Diantha's supreme elegance!"

She shrugged. "I couldn't hope to wear her kind of clothes with any degree of success," she said honestly.

He smiled. "You wear your own kind very successfully," he assured her admiringly . . . and turned to greet the beautiful Diantha who swept into the room in a dress of black velvet, classic in its simplicity and cut by the hand of a master, striking contrast to her gleaming curls and sapphire eyes and perfect, magnolia skin.

Sylvie immediately realized that her own choice of clothes for evening had been a mistake. Her dress was very pretty but much too youthful. She must look like a green girl. Whereas Diantha Craig looked just what she was . . . a beautiful, sophisticated, supremely confident woman who held Edward in the palm of her hand.

It showed in the way that she smiled on him and appropriated his attention without the least effort. It showed in the slightly amused, slightly contemptuous smile that she bestowed on Sylvie in her pretty dress.

It was not just a matter of clothes, Sylvie thought wryly . . . of knowing what to buy and where to buy it and how to wear it. Her own clothes came from a very famous fashion house. It was really a matter of confidence.

Diantha knew all about men and how to attract them, how to hold them. And Edward, like most men, seemed to be too swayed by his senses to realize that she was ambitious rather than loving. Sylvie knew instinctively that the woman meant to marry Edward if she could. She did not love him. She cared nothing for his happiness. She merely wished to be Lady Carluke!

Well, Sylvie did not love him, either. But she found that she did care about his happiness to some extent. He deserved better than a wife like Diantha Craig for all his faults, she thought vehemently.

She might not be beautiful or clever or worldly-wise. She might know nothing of the kind of life he lived and obviously enjoyed. But she was very sure that she could be a good wife to him!

However, it was not at all likely that she would be given the opportunity . . .

# 6

**L**ATER in the week, Edward returned from a meeting with his able but somewhat anxious agent to find Leo on the terrace with Sylvie.

A little frown touched his dark eyes. He paused, studying the couple. Leo was forever about the place of late despite the fact that he was a busy farmer. He did not seem to need that encouragement from his helpful Mama to further an obvious interest in Sylvie, Edward thought dryly.

She was chatting to Leo with an ease and a confidence that she seldom brought to their encounters. At one time, she had seemed inclined to like him, to trust him. He wondered what he had said or done to make her retreat into her shy shell, to take pains to keep out of his way as much as possible.

He knew that he tended to tease her, to treat her like a nice child whose innocence amused rather than appealed. But it was a defensive attitude to prevent himself from thinking of her as a very desirable woman.

Sylvie was very young and totally innocent. It would be wrong to lay siege to her loveliness unless he was prepared to marry her.

He still did not take kindly to the thought of marrying anyone. He enjoyed his freedom. He was not ready to commit himself to one woman when there were so many attractive and willing women in the world. But he thought of that long session with Hammond, his agent. The bills were mounting. A few creditors were pressing. Some repairs were very necessary. Hammond suggested that he sell a portion of his land to salvage his financial situation. But Edward instinctively rebelled against the idea. It was good Carluke land and he had sworn never to part with an acre of it. The property developers who were interested only meant to spoil the landscape with a clutch of modern houses which they would sell at exorbitant prices. And it would only mean a temporary easing of his problems.

He knew that he was fighting a losing battle with the financial demands of the estate. It seemed that he had two choices . . . to sell some of his land or to marry money. Which meant that he had no choice at all, he thought grimly.

Leo rose to shake hands with him and explain his presence. He had met Diantha in the village and brought her back to the Hall by car.

"Diantha walking? I don't believe it." Edward sat down by Sylvie and smiled at her warmly. "That must be your influence!"

She laughed, shook her head. "She wanted to post a parcel to her publisher. I offered to take it but she said that she would be glad of the walk."

"And is stretched out on her bed as a consequence, I daresay."

Diantha came up behind him and laid her hand lightly on his shoulder. "You are quite wrong. I've been changing my shoes."

Edward smiled lazily and raised his hand to clasp the slender fingers. She bent to kiss his cheek. Sylvie glanced away from that affectionate exchange with an instinctive dislike that grew stronger every day. Happening to look at Leo, she saw an expression in his very blue eyes that betrayed his dislike of it, too.

She felt a shock of surprise. She was aware that he had known Diantha for a long time before he had introduced her to Edward. Now she wondered if Leo were in love with Diantha. If so, how it must hurt him that she was staying at the Hall as Edward's guest and, possibly, his future wife! Her warm and compassionate heart went out to him.

He left very soon, refusing an invitation to join them for lunch.

131

Diantha chose to accompany him to his car and they strolled off together, her hand linked in his arm, chatting with the ease of long association.

Left alone with Edward, Sylvie was abruptly aware that she was very scantily clad. She had been sunbathing in the briefest of bikinis, secure in the knowledge that Edward and Diantha were out and that Lady Carluke, feeling a little frailer than usual, had decided to spend the day resting in her room. It was a very hot day for they were enjoying one of those rare settled spells which belies all that is said about English summers.

Leo and Diantha had surprised her by their unexpected appearance. Diantha had gone directly to her room to change her shoes. Sylvie had sat down quite happily with Leo, knowing he was too much of a gentleman to ogle her.

She wished she could say the same for Edward, she thought crossly, the colour rising in her small face as she realized the amused appreciation in his dark eyes.

Her bikini seemed to shrink to minuscule proportions before his gaze. She knew she must escape and she rose from her chair to go to her room.

His hand shot out to catch her by the wrist as she passed him. "Now where are *you* going?" he demanded lightly.

"To dress."

He heaved a mock sigh. "And I have so few pleasures in life," he said mournfully.

Her lips twitched with reluctant laughter. "I wish you wouldn't stare!" she exclaimed impulsively.

"I happen to like the scenery," he told her outrageously, his eyes twinkling. She had not seemed to mind Leo's admiring gaze. He wondered why she should be more conscious of her lovely body when he looked at it. He released her, taking pity on her obvious embarrassment. "I suppose you're wise. I don't think I could concentrate on my lunch with you

133

looking like that!"

When she came down, just in time for the light meal, she had changed into a cool frock of white broderie anglaise cotton. She slipped into her seat and helped herself to cold chicken and salad.

Diantha turned to her with a deceptively sweet smile. "I'm afraid you will ruin your complexion by exposing it to so much sun, my dear. You will be *leathery* by the time you are thirty-five, you know!" She avoided the sun as much as possible, having the very sensitive skin that went with her colouring, and she was rather envious of the girl's glorious tan.

"Virtually all over . . ." Edward murmured softly, pouring the sparkling white wine.

Sylvie shot him a furious glance.

Diantha's eyes narrowed but she continued to smile. "One's *face* is what matters, of course. One doesn't usually expose the body to the world, after all."

"Not in our climate, certainly." Edward's eyes twinkled at Sylvie across the table. "I've often deplored the fact."

The two women exchanged exasperated glances in a brief, age-old unity against the impossible behaviour of the male.

Sylvie said, rather more warmly than usual when talking to a woman she could not like: "I expect I am rather careless of my skin. That comes of spending so much time out of doors, I daresay. And, of course, I'm so lucky that I don't burn."

"So surprising in a blonde," Diantha agreed, quite pleasantly. "I wish I could enjoy the sun. But I'm afraid that I am rather selfishly longing for the weather to break. It's really *too* hot . . . ." She drank a little of her wine. "Edward, have you finished with business for today? Do you think we might go for a drive this afternoon? There's that little place on the coast with all the antique shops that I'd rather like to see again . . . ."

Sylvie turned her attention to the excellent lunch, knowing that she had been dismissed. Diantha Craig seldom wasted much time or energy in talking to her own sex.

She was Edward's friend and Edward's guest and it was very natural that he should spend most of his time in her company, carrying out her wishes and taking her wherever she wished to go. Sylvie knew that she was not included in Diantha's plans for the afternoon. She did not mind at all. There was no pleasure for her in seeing them together and observing how attentive and affectionate and admiring Edward was towards this latest and possibly the last woman in his life.

It was impossible to rid her mind of Lucinda's light words. Apparently the whole world knew that Edward was in such dire financial straits that he would have to marry a wealthy woman. One could not blame him for combining necessity with the affection he obviously felt for Diantha Craig. She must be rich, Sylvie thought bleakly. For her books sold well and sold in many countries.

He was so attentive, so willing to please, that he must be leading up to a proposal of marriage and Sylvie did not doubt that Diantha would leap at it. But would Edward be happy? Sylvie rather fancied that he would have to dance to Diantha's tune for she would certainly hold on to the purse-strings. Surely that would not suit a man who was both proud and sensitive?

Sylvie hated the thought of such a marriage for him. She might not know him very well. She might not always like him. But she responded instinctively to that quickness of mind and spirit, that love of life, that delightful, slightly wicked sense of humour and felt that it would be quenched by life with a woman who did not truly love or understand him. He deserved so much better than the cool, calculating Diantha!

After lunch, she left them to spend

an hour with Lady Carluke. Mutual liking easily bridged the years between them. When her cousin eventually said that she would sleep for a while, Sylvie decided to take a rug and a radio and her sketching things and go down to the lake. It would be cool by the water's edge and she would be shaded from the fierce heat of the afternoon sun by the tall trees.

Hero was drowsing in a quiet corner of the terrace, out of the sun. Sylvie did not disturb her, knowing that the elderly dog was uncomfortable in the heat. There was no sight nor sound of Edward and Diantha and she supposed that they had set off on their expedition to the coast.

It was lovely by the lake. Used to being alone, she was perfectly content. It was very still, very peaceful, and she lost herself in the beauty of her surroundings.

Sketching happily, she looked up to see Edward walking towards her. She frowned for she had managed to forget him temporarily. It troubled her that he was so often in her thoughts. She was in no danger of loving him, of course. But she knew that she was just a little attracted. He was really very good-looking, a most attractive man with a great deal of charm that touched her heart and quickened her pulses. It seemed that one did not need to like a man particularly to be dangerously aware of his physical attractions, she thought wryly. She was rather scared of that swift response in her to his touch, his nearness. Because of it, she had taken pains during the last few days not to be alone with him any more than she could help. She did not wholly trust that sensual streak in him — and she certainly did not trust herself not to betray the excitement that he evoked so easily.

It was only because she had known very few men — and no one at all like him, she told herself sensibly. Being a level-headed girl with much of her father's shrewdness, she knew just how foolish it would be to allow herself to fall really in love with Edward Carluke. For he would never marry her, she knew. All her father's money could not make her attractive to him. He did not want a naïve girl when he might have the mature, sophisticated and very beautiful Diantha Craig . . .

Edward looked down at her, smiling. He thought how charming she looked in the cool cotton frock, refreshingly young and unspoiled. The pale blonde hair framed her face, soft and straight with just the prettiest lift of a curl at the ends. She regarded him coolly. Having extricated himself from Diantha with a little difficulty, he felt that she might have greeted him with greater warmth. Instead he had seen a flicker of dismay in the grey eyes as he walked towards her. He was puzzled. Most women liked him too well. It was something of a challenge that this one did not seem to like him at all and certainly refused to respond to him with the readiness of other women.

He wondered how she would react to a proposal of marriage from him. It was all very well to tell himself that Hugh Waring's daughter could solve all his problems. He fancied that she was the only woman he knew who did not want him for a husband!

But he had always found that a confident approach could win the day. And he did want her, damn it! It wasn't just the money that tempted him . . .

"I thought you might be here," he said lightly.

The words implied that he had been looking for her. Her heart bumped but she merely smiled politely and waited for him to explain.

Edward lowered himself to the grass beside her. "Do I intrude?" He spoke with the easy manner of someone who was usually welcomed with glad cries.

His warm smile was very attractive. Sylvie resisted the temptation to reply as he obviously expected. "Will you go away if I say yes?" she asked, a little dryly.

"No," he said promptly.

"That's what I thought." She set aside her pad and pencil with a faint sigh.

Edward's eyes crinkled. "You ought not to betray so much delight in my company, you know," he said, amused. "I shall begin to believe that you like me."

"That will never do," she agreed lightly.

Encouraged by the glimpse of a smile in her grey eyes, he went on smoothly: "You must learn to like me if we are to be married, you know."

She looked at him swiftly, very startled. "Married . . . ?"

He smiled at her warmly. "I like to please my Mama," he explained, dark eyes dancing.

Her heart steadied. She shook her head at him in amused reproach. "Are you never serious?" she demanded, half-laughing, warming to him just as he had intended. "Take care, Edward!

142

That's the second time that you've bordered on a proposal of marriage and a less scrupulous woman might take you up on it! Fortunately, I know that you haven't the least wish to marry me!"

"You are mistaken," he said quietly, no longer smiling.

Struck by something in his tone, Sylvie stared at him and found that his eyes were intent upon her, very serious. She had begun to believe that it was impossible for him to take anything seriously — and her heart suffered a severe shock.

The colour drained from her face, leaving it white beneath the tan. She rose swiftly to her feet, alarmed. So did Edward. She put out a hand as though to ward him off although he had made no move towards her. "How — how absurd," she said shakily. "You know scarcely anything about me!"

His lips twitched. "I could have a great time finding out all about you," he said confidently. "Wouldn't you like to marry me, Sylvie?"

Now his eyes were dancing again and his tone was light. It was impossible to believe that he meant the words. "No, I wouldn't," she declared firmly.

"You're the only woman I know who could say that and mean it, I suspect," he told her with his mocking, light-hearted arrogance.

"I do mean it!"

"I know you do. What have I done to give you such a dislike of me, I wonder?" he mused.

Sylvie felt oddly compelled to protest. "I don't dislike you," she murmured.

"Then you don't trust me? Is that it?" His tone was rueful.

Sylvie hesitated, not quite sure if he was in earnest. Surely he could not really be seriously thinking of asking her to marry him!

She moved away from him to the water's edge and looked across the lake at the beautiful Cumbrian hills. "I distrust your motives," she said as lightly as she could for her hammering heart.

"My motives? I imagine they must be obvious," he said with disarming candour. "I'm desperately short of money and you're a millionaire's daughter!"

Turning swiftly, indignant, Sylvie saw the devilry in his glowing eyes. She relaxed, quivering with reluctant laughter. She might have known that he was only teasing her, as usual. She was relieved. At the same time, she felt just a twinge of regret . . . .

"It seems a one-sided bargain," she said dryly. "I wonder how I would benefit from such a marriage?"

He raised an amused eyebrow. "But you get me, of course. What more could a woman want?"

She smiled at him. "I'm not tempted."

He heaved a mock sigh. "My Mama will be so disappointed."

"I'm sure she doesn't wish you to marry any girl in cold blood," she said firmly.

"Cold blood?" he echoed. "You underestimate your attractions, my sweet!"

Sylvie glanced at him doubtfully. But there was a genuine admiration in the dark eyes and she was woman enough to be warmed by it. At the same time, she realized the dangers of responding in any way that could be construed as encouragement.

"I don't underestimate the attractions of my father's bank balance," she said dryly, the smile in her eyes taking all sting from the words. She began to gather her scattered possessions. "It must be time for tea, don't you think?"

Edward agreed, wisely deciding to say no more for the moment. He found it discouragingly hard to believe that he could persuade the level-headed Sylvie into marriage. For, as she pointed out, how did she benefit? She was not like other girls who fell in love with him with very little encouragement. He was not even sure that she liked him. She seemed to like Leo very much better, he thought wryly . . .

And thought it again that evening as he watched her dancing in Leo's arms at the Country Club. She looked very pretty in floating lilac chiffon and her face was raised to Leo in laughing delight as he whirled her about the floor to the music.

There was a warmth in Leo's eyes that made Edward wonder if his serious friend were falling in love at last. It would be too ironic if Leo should want the one girl that he so desperately needed to marry to prevent his estate from dwindling.

She might have been engaged to him now if he had not handled matters so badly that afternoon, he told himself ruefully. It seemed that his usual confidence had deserted him when it came to proposing marriage to a woman for the first time in his life. Or had he just been deterred by her seeming indifference to the charm that had won so many women in the past?

Lucinda leaned towards him. "They look well together, don't they?" She liked Sylvie and it was nice to see Leo looking so relaxed and happy. He worked hard and did not devote enough time to pleasure, she felt . . . and he had seemed to be rather depressed during the last few days. He had not confided in her but she suspected that a woman was to blame. So she was particularly pleased to see him taking an interest in someone else.

"Sorry . . . ?" Edward reined his wandering thoughts.

"Leo and Sylvie. I like her so much, don't you? She's the only girl that I've really felt would be right for him," she added with sisterly concern.

"Is he thinking of marrying her?" Diantha was rather more interested than her careless tone implied. She had turned Leo down but it did not suit her that he should find someone to take her place. She knew she should be thankful that the girl was more interested in Leo than in Edward who might be very tempted by the Waring wealth. But she viewed the obvious warmth between Leo and Sylvie Waring with a slight uneasiness.

"Oh, Leo doesn't talk to me about his love affairs," Lucinda said lightly, unaware that she was talking to the one love of her brother's life. "But he's spending an awful lot of his time at the Hall since he met her and they do seem to be on very affectionate terms."

Sylvie and Leo had become very good friends in the short time that they had known each other. But they had liked each other at first meeting. Because there was no sentiment in that mutual liking they were entirely at ease with each other. It did not seem to either of them that anyone could misconstrue their pleasure in each other's company. They were friends and surely that must be obvious to the whole world.

Leo would have been gratified to know that Diantha disliked his attentiveness to the youthful Sylvie Waring. Drawn like a moth to the flame, he consciously used his friendship with the pretty girl so that he might see more of the woman who had hurt him so badly months before. Time had not eased his hurt or lessened his love. Diantha was still as dear to him, still as necessary to his happiness — and she was even more unattainable, it seemed. He was living in constant dread of hearing that she meant to marry Edward. It was painful to him to see them together. But he could not stay away.

Quite unconsciously, Sylvie was using him, too. She needed a camouflage for the growing interest in Edward that threatened to over-rule her cautious head and engage her impulsive heart. She did not want him to suspect how much he affected her emotions. It was not enough to keep him at a careful distance. She must convince him of her indifference. How better than a seeming preference for the company and the attentions of a man who was no threat at all to her peace of mind? And, having surprised that look in Leo's eyes, she was very sure that he was in need of the little comfort that her liking and affection might give.

So she smiled on him warmly and responded with eager animation to his light remarks and gave herself up to the pleasure of dancing with such a good partner and firmly forbore to glance at Edward to see if he noticed or cared that she was enjoying herself so well with his friend.

She knew perfectly well that Edward only had eyes for the beautiful Diantha, after all. She could not hope to compete with her for his interest. She did not wish to compete, she told herself firmly.

Yet her heart sank when Leo escorted her back to the table and she saw that Edward laughed in response to something Diantha said and reached to cover the woman's hand with his own and smiled into the lovely sapphire eyes with meaningful warmth.

Sylvie felt a sharp, unaccountable pain in her breast like a twisting knife and knew a very foolish inclination to burst into tears.

Then Edward rose to his feet before she could resume her seat and stepped forward, saying lightly, confidently: "My turn, I think."

Before she could say yea or nay, he had swept her out to the dance floor and she was held firmly in his arms.

# 7

HER heart was pounding so hard that she thought he must hear it. He held her too close for comfort, his cheek firmly pressed against her own. He danced superbly but Sylvie could not relax and enjoy moving in his arms to the music. Much too conscious of him, her body responding involuntarily to the nearness of him, she was fighting hard to keep her composure.

"You're getting on very well with Leo," he said, almost accusing. "I think I'm jealous."

Sylvie forced a smile. "I think you are nonsensical."

"But you do like him."

"Very much. I've no reason to dislike him," she countered. "He is very pleasant, very friendly, very nice to me."

153

"While I am unpleasant, unfriendly and very nasty?" he suggested, eyes twinkling.

It would be so much easier to resist him if he were, she thought ruefully. In truth, he was a charmer who seemed to have the power to take possession of her heart.

"You know that you aren't." It was an impulsive and quite involuntary retort with a hint of rue in it.

"Then you should like me, too," he told her firmly.

"If you insist," she said, shrugging her slim shoulders.

Edward was enchanted by the careless answer. He laughed softly. He looked down at her, liking her. The music was slow, sensuous. Their steps matched very well. Almost unconsciously, his arms closed more firmly about her slight figure. She was a delight to hold and he suddenly ached to kiss her, to coax her into the response that she continued to withhold so resolutely.

He did not pause to ask himself if it

154

was only the challenge of her apparent indifference or if she was really more appealing and more attractive to him than any of the women he had known in the past.

He steered her through an open window and out to a secluded balcony that was very popular but chanced to be deserted at that particular moment. Sylvie raised a startled face. He smiled reassuringly.

"No!" she exclaimed, recognizing the glow of intent in his eyes.

"Yes," he said, determined. He did not suspect her of coquetry but he was tired of being held at arm's length. He ached to hold her, to kiss her, to make love to her. He wanted her as he had seldom wanted any woman.

She tried to pull away. His arm tightened purposefully about her. "Edward . . . !" she warned with a hint of desperation, afraid that the first touch of his mouth on her own would unleash that wild fire within her and that he would know it.

"Sylvie . . . !" he said, gently mocking, very sure of himself. "I mean to kiss you so don't fight me." He brushed a strand of soft hair from her face.

Apprehension sharpened. "I wish you would be sensible! Keep your kisses for those who want them — I certainly don't!"

He smiled down at her with that little imp of devilry in his eyes. "Don't you?" His tone was soft, seductive. Tantalizingly, his lips almost brushed her mouth.

Her lips quivered in anticipation. She jerked her head away from him, furious with herself. "You're despicable!" she flared. "Don't you know how badly you are behaving? Everyone knows what you are and why you've hustled me out here — and it must seem that I'm willing!"

He raised an eyebrow. "What makes you so cross? What's a kiss or two between friends?" His eyes and his voice held faint amusement. "Are you afraid that Leo won't like it if I kiss you?"

"*I* won't like it!" she said swiftly, hotly.

"I promise that you will," he returned, very quietly and with unmistakable meaning. He bent his dark head and kissed the soft mouth with a gentleness that few women had ever known in him. Her lips were cold, refusing to respond. Edward knew a flicker of disappointment but decided that pride rather than indifference stood between them. She had a great deal of spirit and he admired that. He curbed the impulse to kiss her again. The time, the place and the mood were all against him. He let her go. "Well?"

Her chin tilted. "I *didn't* like it."

He smiled. "Nor did I, my dear. Kissing is like quarrelling — it takes two!"

It had taken all Sylvie's strength of mind to resist the hint of magic in that kiss. She had longed to melt into his arms, to give herself to the delight and the dawning of desire. Now, feeling reproached, she knew a very foolish regret that she had rebuffed him and realized that she would need to keep a firm rein on her inexperienced heart. He was much too attractive!

"I don't quarrel with men I scarcely know, either," she said, tart.

Edward laughed. "You lead a very dull life, my sweet."

Sylvie stiffened. "Anyone's life must seem dull in comparison to the one that you lead!"

He shrugged. "I like a little excitement, I must admit. But a man has to sow a few wild oats before he settles down, you know. I daresay I shall be a reformed character once I am married." He spoke smoothly but his eyes danced with mischief.

Sylvie's heart jumped. But her chin tilted. It was no longer such an amusing game, she decided crossly. "First catch your bride!" she said haughtily.

"I can name a dozen girls who would marry me," he said with the infuriating confidence that irritated her so much because she could not doubt the claim. "But not one of them has just the right qualities that I'm looking for in a wife."

"Like a wealthy father, for instance?" she suggested sweetly.

"Like a *very* wealthy father," he amended coolly.

Sylvie felt a pang. He was too honest for comfort. She would be mad to marry a man who made no secret of his motive for wanting her. But, to be fair to him, he had not yet asked her to marry him in all seriousness — and she hoped he did not mean to do so. For she could not trust herself to give the right and sensible answer. Against her will, she felt more and more drawn to him . . .

"It isn't just the money, of course," he added soothingly, eyes twinkling. "I quite like you, too."

"Well, I don't like *you* — and nothing could induce me to marry you," she declared, almost defiant.

He shook his head at her in gentle reproach. "It's good manners to wait until you're asked, my sweet."

"Oh, ask! Let's get the wretched business over and done with!" She did not mean to sound so cross, so impatient. But she was stupidly hurt by the cold-blooded pursuit and suddenly weary of the teasing that probably had its roots in serious intent, after all.

All the laughter fled from his eyes. He looked down at her intently, something in his gaze that she could not analyse but which made her feel slightly uncomfortable. He smiled without warmth. "I mustn't embarrass you with a proposal that is so obviously unwelcome," he said lightly. "My Mama will just have to be disappointed."

He escorted her back to their table and Sylvie tried not to feel swamped by her own foolish feeling of disappointment. She marvelled at the perversity of her emotions. She did not seem to know what she did want!

Leo and Diantha left the dance floor

at the same time. His arm was still about her waist and she smiled at him with warmth. She had been fluid in his arms and there was a hint of their former relationship in the way that she responded to him, Leo felt. He might have allowed himself to be optimistic if she had not turned so promptly at the sound of Edward's voice.

Relinquishing her, he fell into step with Sylvie, a wry expression in his blue eyes. She slipped her hand round his arm in an instinctive gesture of compassion and, if she but realized it, a seeking after comfort for herself. For her heart had sunk when she was deserted so cavalierly for the beautiful Diantha Craig. Perhaps she had slapped Edward down a little too hard, she thought ruefully . . .

Leo smiled on her with very real liking and a growing affection and covered her slender fingers with his own. "All right, Sylvie? Enjoying the evening?"

"Very much," she said brightly.

*Parts of it*, she amended silently, her gaze on Edward's broad back and handsome head as he walked through the tables with Diantha clinging to his arm.

Glancing over his shoulder, Edward observed the little exchange of words and warm smiles, all the implication of mutual affection. He felt a stab of something that might have been jealousy — but was much more likely to be irritation because she continued to rebuff him as plainly as she smiled on his friend, he told himself firmly.

He did not underestimate Leo's attractiveness, the integrity and warmth that must appeal to any woman. It was possible that Sylvie was rapidly falling in love — and that would certainly put paid to his hope of marrying her. If he wanted her, he must move fast to secure her, obviously. But the charm and the personality and the tactics that had always won him what he wanted in the past did not seem to have much impact on Sylvie, he thought with a hint of impatience. She had a very cool head on those pretty shoulders and a heart that she obviously did not mean to place in his keeping.

Perhaps he should dismiss the odd fancy that she was the kind of wife that he wanted — if he must marry at all . . .

It seemed to Sylvie that he was a very devoted and attentive lover during the following days . . . and Diantha almost purred with satisfaction. The woman was so sure of him that she might be wearing his ring, Sylvie thought wryly, refusing to look too closely into her dislike of the situation.

It seemed that Edward had thought better of his lighthearted teasing, his pretend pursuit — and she was thankful for it. He was courteous, pleasant — and just a little distant. She refused to mind.

It seemed that he had made up his mind to marry Diantha, after all. Of course he had never been serious about proposing to her! Even her father's money could not make her attractive to a man like Edward, in truth. She should be relieved that he had ceased to tease her. But as the days passed and his mother and friends obviously expected him to announce his engagement to Diantha at any moment, her heart grew heavier.

She was not in love with him. She had no wish to marry a man who was little more than a stranger. But she did like him more than she had thought possible at first meeting — and he had awoken new and disturbing emotions that ached for fulfilment in his arms. But she had rejected every overture and she had only herself to blame if he had tired of the game. If it had not been so obviously a game to him, she might not have rejected him so forcefully. It was a vicious circle, she thought, sighing.

She was very grateful for Leo's undemanding friendship and quiet support. It was a balm for her pride that she could refuse obviously dutiful invitations from Edward on the grounds that she was riding with Leo, driving with Leo, playing tennis with Leo, having lunch or dinner with Leo . . . and never once did he give her any reason to suppose that he objected to her growing intimacy with his friend.

But very often they were a foursome — and then she was even more thankful to rely on Leo's unfailing attentiveness to ease the hurt of Edward's marked interest in someone else. He talked and laughed and made light love to Diantha with eye and voice and the dark head was often very close to those bright curls. They were a very attractive couple. Sylvie heard it said too many times.

She had tried to like Diantha and failed. The woman patronized her, emphasising her youth and lack of sophistication at every turn. She was much too sure of herself . . . and of Edward! She seemed to flaunt their intimacy and her hold of his affections all the time. Sylvie supposed that it was for her benefit more than anything else. Being a woman, Diantha probably sensed that she liked Edward rather too much for peace of mind!

One evening, returning from a dinner party at Rylands, she was in the back of the car while Edward drove along the quiet roads with Diantha by his side.

Diantha was talkative, stimulated by wine and flattery and the excitement of the evening, and Edward was obviously in a mood to be amused and entertained. Observing his response to everything that Diantha said and did, Sylvie wondered that she had ever doubted his love for the woman.

Her heart sank unaccountably.

She tried to escape to her room when they reached the Hall. Edward suggested a nightcap and, sweeping aside her protest, ushered her into the drawing-room with Diantha. He gave her a drink that she really did not want and smiled at her with greater warmth in his dark eyes than she had seen for some days. Her foolish heart leaped.

He turned away immediately as

Diantha spoke to him. Sylvie nursed her drink, pretending to listen to the conversation and smiling politely whenever they remembered to include her in it. She could not help feeling that she intruded on the precious intimacy of lovers as they sat side by side on the long sofa.

Sylvie wondered if he deliberately stressed the warmth and strength of his feeling for another woman. Did he suspect her dislike and foolish jealousy of the relationship?

Oh, she did not really care if they were lovers or if they meant to marry, she told herself firmly. But a sudden vision of them in close and passionate embrace, of Diantha walking confidently down the aisle as his bride, was suddenly so painful that she was forced to admit that she cared very much indeed!

Her heart stood still with shock. It was quite absurd and very foolish but it seemed that she was halfway to being in love with Edward Carluke. And all because he had smiled, paid her a little teasing attention, charmed her as he had charmed too many women in his thirty-odd years!

Diantha rose and went to the piano and lifted the lid. She began to play a popular ballad from a musical that she and Edward had recently seen together. He walked across the room to stand by the piano, smiling, affection and admiration in his dark eyes.

Diantha was so lovely and he was so obviously a lover that Sylvie's heart abruptly swelled with an intolerable anguish.

She put down her untouched drink and got to her feet, tears sparkling on her long, dark lashes. She desperately needed to escape to the sanctuary of her room, leaving the lovers to their glowing delight in each other, so that she could come to terms with this strange and unwelcome upheaval of her emotions.

Edward looked at her across the room. For a moment, their eyes met and held. Her gaze was bright, almost defiant. Suddenly he saw that proud chin quiver like a child's — and he wondered if she was near to tears . . . and why?

She had been quiet since they left Rylands. Casting his mind back, he could not think of anything to account for her seeming depression. Leo had been even more attentive than usual and Sylvie had seemed to enjoy herself. He had observed Leo's increasing affection and Sylvie's obvious response with a hint of annoyance.

The easy conquest of too many women had spoiled him. So he had been irritated when Sylvie refused to be impressed by the charm that other women found so irresistible.

He had decided to shrug his shoulders and forget her. Diantha was available and willing and only waiting for him to suggest marriage. Why shouldn't he marry her? She had almost as much to offer as Hugh Waring's daughter!

But he had discovered that Sylvie

was not so easily dismissed. That had irritated him, too. He liked to be in control of every situation. But she had begun to intrude into his thoughts when he least wanted or expected it. He had begun to depend on her presence and her smiles for his enjoyment of each day.

Now he admitted that he wanted to marry her. It had nothing to do with loving, of course. Edward knew all about loving and its demands. It was liking that would last. It was admiration and approval. It was desire that was touched with a new kind of tenderness — and his male pride insisted that it should find some response before he mentioned marriage to her.

But she only seemed to respond to Leo, he thought with sudden impatience. Leo was a good friend and he wished him well. He also wished him a million miles away! For he was a definite obstacle in Edward's path to the altar.

Perhaps it was time for a change of

tactics if he did not wish to lose her to his friend . . .

Edward smiled, held out his hand. "The last waltz," he said lightly. "Dance it with me before you run away to bed."

Surprised, reluctant for his embrace however innocent of amorous intent, Sylvie glanced at Diantha, expecting her to come to the rescue. For she would surely object.

But, obviously secure in the belief that she had Edward just where she wanted him and could afford to be generous to a young and rather silly girl who was infatuated with her man, Diantha smiled and nodded approval and continued to play the dreamy ballad.

Knowing it was foolish, Sylvie went into the waiting arms. She needed to be close to him, however briefly. It was stupid to feel grateful but he had been a little distant during the last week or so and now she was relieved by the friendliness in the dark eyes, by the comforting way that his arms closed about her slight body.

Her heart was suddenly very full — and she hoped that he did not know it. But she suspected that he did. He was much too perceptive — and much too sure of his impact on a woman's emotions . . .

It had been a mistake, Edward instantly knew. He wanted her in his arms but not under Diantha's too-watchful gaze. Holding her was too much temptation!

She was stiff, self-conscious, unusually ill-at-ease. He wished he knew if it was response or resentment that quickened the rise and fall of the lovely breasts. He wished he knew just what was in her mind and heart.

The soft scent of her hair, the light perfume she wore and the appealing femininity of her body evoked desire . . . and something that went beyond the physical need of a man for a woman. He felt very tender, very caring towards her . . . and it surprised him.

172

She could become much too important to him, he suddenly realized — and wondered if he should draw back before it was too late. For she seemed determined not to care for him.

It took all his strength of mind to prevent the light and impersonal hold from turning into a warm embrace. But he could not resist the temptation to touch his lips to the mass of pale hair that framed her face.

Sylvie was shaken by that light kiss and highly suspicious of a man who blew hot and then cold so unaccountably that a woman could never know what he really felt or intended!

She stumbled over his feet for a third time and broke away from him, forcing a smile for the benefit of the watching Diantha. "Sorry. I'm trampling you to death," she said as lightly as she could. "I think I'd better go to bed. I'm too tired to concentrate."

Diantha rose and closed the piano lid. She moved to Edward's side and linked her hand in his arm, smiling at him with her usual, glowing confidence.

"I'm ready to go up, too, darling. It is getting late."

Perhaps the words were innocent of any invitation but Sylvie found that her hands clenched so fiercely at the woman's words that the nails dug tiny crescents into the palms.

She wished them a careful goodnight and left them together, refusing to dwell on the likelihood that they would spend the rest of the night locked in each other's loving arms. She had known from the first that they were lovers. Why should it hurt more now than then?

Even as she turned away, Diantha reached to put her arms about Edward's neck. Sylvie did not wait to observe his reactions. She was much too concerned with her own, a tidal wave of resentment that was quite shocking in its intensity. She discovered that jealousy could be very painful and very ugly . . .

Edward kissed Diantha, very briefly, and extricated himself from that possessive embrace. He had no heart for making light love to her and he instinctively disliked her growing confidence in the outcome of their affair.

She was very lovely, very desirable. But he suddenly found that he no longer desired her at all. He had been stirred so deeply by the virginal reluctance of an inexperienced girl that he was quite unable to respond to Diantha's warm and overt and practised sensuality.

Diantha was not disturbed by the impersonal kiss, the faint air of dismissal in his attitude. She was too sure of his intentions. She knew that he would probably ask her to marry him before she went back to London at the end of the week.

She had made up her mind to refuse him. Some men were born to be lovers. They did not make very good husbands. She felt that Edward came into that category.

Diantha was very fond of him but the man she eventually married would need to be loyal and reliable and continually caring — and she had failed to find those qualities during the months that she had known him. He was spoiled and selfish and sensual and very fickle — and not at all in love with her, she suspected. Marriage was merely a matter of expediency for him and no doubt he regarded her as a very suitable bride, she thought dryly.

He played the part of lover very well but a woman always knew when a man's heart was not involved in the relationship. She suspected that Edward was incapable of loving any woman other than lightly and very carelessly.

She had enjoyed their affair but she felt it was almost time to end it. For Edward seemed to be seriously in pursuit of a convenient marriage to solve his financial difficulties — and she did not mean to be married for such reasons.

Idly, she wondered if he would turn to the youthful Sylvie Waring as a second choice. It would please his mother. No doubt it would please Hugh Waring who would probably care more for Edward's title and estates than his reputation.

As for the girl . . . well, she was very young and no one knew better than Edward how to coax a woman into giving him what he wanted!

But there might be an obstacle.

The girl seemed to be very fond of Leo — and might even be falling in love with him. The growing conviction that Leo was very fond of Sylvie had caused a certain disquiet in Diantha's mind and heart for some days . . .

# 8

LEFT alone, Edward sat down at the piano so recently vacated by Diantha and allowed his hands to stray lightly and absently over the keys. He wanted to think and he had always found that music was an aid to concentration.

He had been rather shaken to realize how much he wished to marry Sylvie. He had supposed that he was contemplating marriage in cold blood and he had taken every opportunity offered to compare her with Diantha in recent days. Comparisons might be odious but a man had to know what he was doing when it came to the serious business of matrimony, he had told himself firmly.

In many ways, Diantha seemed the ideal choice of bride for a man like himself. But he had decided that she was too superficial. A man wanted warmth and integrity and sweetness in the woman he married. He felt that Sylvie possessed those qualities in full measure. Diantha was fickle, too — much sought after by men. A man wanted to feel that he would always be the only one of importance to his wife. Edward felt that Sylvie would be a loyal and loving wife for any man.

He had discovered that she was enchanting, a constant delight to him with her shy modesty and her direct candour and her warm, sweet smile with all its hint of a generous and lovable nature. He had suddenly and unexpectedly discovered that he wanted very much to marry her. But could he persuade her to marry him?

For the first time in his life, Edward dreaded the thought that a woman he wanted might slip through his hands and into another man's arms. Before, no woman had mattered so much that he cared if he lost her to someone else.

Sylvie was different. He did not want to lose her and certainly not to Leo although he admitted with a rare humility that his friend would make a much better husband than himself.

For the first time in his life, he felt that he had little to offer that a girl like Sylvie would think important. She was obviously not impressed by his title or his estates, his looks or his charm . . . and he knew that his reputation was against him.

Women like Diantha considered it to be an added attraction. But to Sylvie, all wide-eyed innocence and charming unsophistication, he was a shocking rake and a care-for-nobody who sought only his own sensual gratification in life, he thought wryly, knowing that she did not trust him. He was very much afraid that she did not even like him!

For the first time in his life, he was very near to loving and it was suddenly vital that he should move quickly to secure what he wanted before he lost it completely.

Perhaps he should attempt to seduce Sylvie into an engagement as soon as possible and concern himself with coaxing her into loving at a later date!

Making his way along the corridor to his own suite of rooms some minutes later, he saw a light showing beneath the door of Sylvie's small sitting-room and halted in his tracks. No better time than the present to talk to her, perhaps, he decided impulsively — and knocked lightly and without hesitation . . .

Sylvie's emotions were in such turmoil that she knew she could not sleep. Having undressed and loosened her hair, she wrapped her slim body in a thin silk robe and curled up on the low window-seat before the open window and tried to come to terms with the confusion of heart and mind.

The night was very warm and quite airless. She opened the window wider and lifted the heavy hair from her neck with both hands, longing for a cool breeze, wondering if she should have gone for a walk in the garden or the grounds despite the late hour. The house seemed filled with Edward's presence and she was desperately trying to close her mind to thoughts of him in Diantha's welcoming arms.

The moon was hiding behind a bank of cloud and there did not seem to be any stars. Sylvie stared at the velvety night and tried to convince herself that it was right and sensible to leave the Hall while her heart was still more or less her own.

She did not wish to go away. Foolishly, she wanted to be near to a man whose slightest smile could catch at her heart. But she suspected that there might be a great deal of heartache in store for her if she stayed and allowed herself to love a man like Edward Carluke.

Deep in thought, she was startled by the light knock at the door. Puzzled and a little apprehensive, she rose and went to answer. At sight of Edward, she drew her robe more closely about her body and realized too late that the instinctively defensive gesture emphasized that it was her only covering.

Edward was too much a man to be unaware of the appeal of those deeply disturbing lines of her slender body beneath the clinging silk. But the impact of the pale hair tumbling about her flower-like face and the widening of those lovely grey eyes in surprise was much more disturbing.

"I saw your light shining beneath the door," he said without preliminary. "May I come in for a few moments?" He smiled at her, very cool and very sure of himself for all the unaccustomed thudding of his heart.

"It's late," Sylvie demurred, startled by the request — and by the fact that he was standing at the door of her room when she had supposed him to be locked in Diantha's embrace.

"Can't we dispense with convention? You aren't in bed and I do want to talk to you."

Sylvie looked at him doubtfully. His

tone was gentle and she fancied there was kindliness in his smile. For one awful moment, she wondered if he knew how she reacted to him and meant to warn her against caring too much. For he could be kind, she knew. But his next words dispelled the anxiety.

"I haven't had five minutes alone with you for days," he said lightly. "Leo monopolizes you — and Diantha does her best to monopolize me! At other times . . . well, I rather think that you are avoiding me, Sylvie."

She was suddenly very much on the defensive, her heart quickening with a familiar apprehension. "I don't know what you have to say to me that the whole world cannot hear!"

A little mischief dawned in his dark eyes. "But you must know that a man likes privacy when he proposes, Sylvie," he chided gently.

His droll tone and the smile allayed her suspicions. He was teasing, as usual. It was an indication that they were friends once more and she was foolishly thankful. The slight barrier between them had worried her more than she cared to admit. She had felt that she had rebuffed him a little too forcibly even if it was only an absurd game.

"I wish you wouldn't be so ridiculous," she said lightly, relaxing, allowing him into the room.

"You are determined not to believe that my intentions are strictly honourable." He sighed. "I suppose I must admit the truth. I really want to make mad, passionate love to you, my sweet." His tone was very light, the dark eyes dancing.

Sylvie laughed, reassured. "More of your nonsense! You don't mean a word of it! It's just a game that you like to play, Edward. I'm afraid I spoil sport by refusing to play it with you."

For answer, he pulled her almost roughly into his arms and kissed her, hard and urgent. Sylvie was roused to instant and alarming response at the touch of his lips, the strength of his arms. She thrust him away before it was betrayed by the treachery of her mouth beneath his own.

"Edward!" she reproached, startled, slightly shocked by the hint of passion in his kiss. He ought not to kiss her in such a way when he was in love with another woman, she thought, disliking evidence of his reputed inability to be faithful to any of his loves.

He was unrepentant. "I never resist that kind of challenge, my sweet."

She looked at him with a hint of indignation in her grey eyes. "It wasn't meant to be a challenge!"

His smile deepened. "I forget how very young you are," he said gently.

Sylvie coloured. She moved away from him, sat down on the sofa and covered her legs carefully with her robe. "Young, yes . . . but not as green as you seem to believe!" she said coolly. "You're just an opportunist."

His eyes danced. "Not exactly," he drawled. "That implies that I wait for opportunities and then make the most of them. In fact, I create the opportunities . . . and you are really quite irresistible, you know."

"Oh, Edward — you don't want me!" she said, suddenly impatient.

He looked down at her. Then he said quietly, with urgent and unmistakable meaning: "You *are* green if you don't know how much I want you!"

Shaken, she stared across the room at him, not knowing whether to be delighted or dismayed by the look in his eyes and the throb of passionate sincerity in his tone.

"I think you'd better go to bed, Edward," she said uncertainly, wondering if he were just a little drunk.

He smiled wryly. "Don't be nervous, my sweet. I won't harm a hair of your pretty head." He moved across the room to her and sat down by her side. "I'd like to make mad, passionate love to you, of course," he added lightly. "And I will . . . but not just yet." He laid his long fingers against her soft cheek in an unmistakable caress.

The promise of the words and the touch of his hand sent a quiver of excitement rippling down her spine and she melted with sudden longing. But she was afraid to trust the sensual and very experienced man who had loved and discarded too many women.

Perhaps he did want her. But she must not allow herself to be flattered because it could only be the kind of wanting that too many other women had evoked in him. If she were foolish enough to weaken and melt into his arms, he would only take all that she was willing to give and walk away when he was bored. For it seemed that no woman lasted very long in Edward Carluke's life . . . not even the beautiful Diantha that Sylvie had felt that he must love.

If he loved Diantha how could he be here with her, making the lightest of love to her with his eyes, his voice, his enchanting smile, offering a promise for the future? Her impulsive heart longed to read a great deal of meaning into his behaviour. Her practical head insisted that it was only flattery for a very obvious purpose. Diantha was a very beautiful woman and no doubt he did love her — but she was not Hugh Waring's daughter!

She forced her slight body to stiffen in defiance of that involuntary shaft of desire. "I wish you would take no for an answer," she said, a little sharply. "I won't be added to the long list of your women!"

"My reputation is my worst enemy," he said, smiling.

"I don't believe it worries you!"

"Not at all — and I must admit that I've thoroughly enjoyed giving the world something to talk about all these years," he drawled, eyes twinkling.

She could not help smiling in response to the wicked amusement that illumined his attractive face. He might be a rake and a rogue but his love of life touched some responsive chord deep in her being.

"So have the women who've helped me to build that reputation," he added softly, quite outrageously, encouraged by her smile.

Sylvie laughed involuntarily.

She was suddenly and quite enchantingly lovely with the merriment dancing in the wide grey eyes. Edward was sure all over again that this was the girl he must marry — if she could be persuaded to have him!

He ached to kiss her, to hold the slight body very close to him. He said carefully, very cool, sounding much more confident than he actually felt: "I wish you would trust me, Sylvie. I'm not trying to seduce you. I'm going to marry you."

The coolly confident announcement took her by surprise . . . and infuriated her. For he made no mention of loving and took no account of her feelings in the matter. Highly indignant, she did not even pause to wonder if he meant the words. "You certainly are not!" she declared stoutly.

190

Her lack of hesitation was commendable in view of the fact that her foolish heart was furious with the practical head that ignored its urgent prompting to take him up on that declaration of intent.

Edward had not expected immediate agreement. She had too much spirit. He smiled at her, very sure of himself. "You've forgotten that women don't say no to me, Sylvie."

"*I* do!"

"I've noticed." His tone was dry but his smile deepened. "I shall persist, you know — and I *always* get my own way."

"You are thoroughly spoiled, in fact," she retorted lightly, refusing to take him seriously. "Well, you won't get your own way this time!" Her head was high despite the hammering of her startled heart and the swift coursing of the blood in her veins.

Edward stifled his own doubts. "I think I will," he said quietly, very confident.

Sylvie stared at him, incredulous. He was in earnest! She was shaken, much too ready to seize the opportunity he offered.

She reminded herself with a fierce upsurge of pride that his proposal was only prompted by the most mercenary of motives and was not even sweetened by a pretence of caring.

"You don't *wish* to marry me," she said, reproaching him for his cold-blooded approach to a very emotive subject.

"But I do."

His tone, the look in his dark eyes, spoke of implacable resolution. Having determined on a course of action, he obviously meant to carry it out . . . and Sylvie felt a little flicker of apprehension that she might be swept into marrying him almost against her will.

"But you don't love me at all," she said flatly and it was blunt statement rather than a question.

Edward hesitated. He would not lie

to her and he was far from sure that the feeling she evoked, so unlike anything he had ever known, could be truly described as loving. He was far from ready to commit himself so irrevocably.

"I like you very well," he said gently. "Liking lasts, Sylvie. I don't know that loving does."

"Your kind of loving is very short-lived, certainly!" Sylvie spoke impulsively, rather scornfully. For she had been a little hurt by his hesitation and disappointed by the insipid offer of liking that was poor comfort for a heart that longed to be loved.

Edward raised a quizzical eyebrow. "I've yet to be convinced that there's any other kind, my sweet."

At least he was honest, she thought wryly. And his words made her pause and look with honesty at her feeling for him. It was excitement. It was longing. It was mingled pain and pleasure. But was it loving?

He knew so much more than she

did about relationships between men and women. Perhaps it was very naive to cling to the romantic belief in a kind of loving that transcended the merely physical . . . and perhaps the way she felt about Edward was only sexual attraction, a fleeting and very foolish infatuation. It was much too soon to be sure that she would love him all her life and beyond . . .

Unless she loved, she could not marry him, she told herself sternly. And if she would not marry him then she had to leave Chase Hall and go home and try to forget all about the man who had stirred her to new and exciting and deeply disturbing emotions.

He covered the hands that were folded so tightly in her lap. "I'm sure we could be very happy without the doubtful blessing of so-called love," he said quietly. "We won't expect too much and we won't hurt and disappoint each other in the way that lovers always do."

She looked at him, very troubled.

"It's so cold-blooded."

He smiled. "It's practical. It won't be at all cold-blooded, I promise."

She tingled at the unmistakable meaning behind the words. Her body quickened with desire for him, a flood of emotion that left her weak. "I can't marry you," she said, a little desperately, feeling that she stood on shifting sand. There was something so ruthless about him that she felt she might find herself at the altar before she knew it! Or was it only that she was much too tempted to resist all that he offered?

"But you will." His dark eyes were warm, smiling, brimming with confidence.

"Oh, you're impossible!" she declared, trying to be angry with him and melting before the warmth of that enchanting smile.

He held both her hands in a firm clasp and looked deep into the wide, candid eyes that betrayed the confusion of her feelings. "Too impossible? I would try very hard to make you happy." He was too wise to make any firm promise. He knew himself much too well.

Sylvie was not the first woman to be swayed by something quite irresistible in his eyes, his smile, his touch.

She was only twenty and she hovered on the threshold of loving a man who knew just how to coax a woman into caring for him. Every fibre of her being yearned for the greatest happiness that a woman could know this side of heaven . . . to love and to know that she was loved. In that moment, drowning in the promise of delight in his dark eyes, she believed that she might find it in his arms.

Trembling, her heart thudding, scarcely knowing what she did for the magic of the moment, she leaned against him and touched her lips to the warm, sensual, slightly smiling mouth. It was a surrender to the inevitable.

Edward caught his breath. Then he put both his arms about her slight body. Holding her close, feeling the throb of her heart through the thin silk robe, tantalizingly aware of firm young breasts thrusting against his chest, he kept a tight rein on the surging excitement that she evoked. He kissed her, very gently. There was the promise of mutual ecstasy in her surprisingly eager response and Edward found it very hard to break away, to resist the unconscious enticement in her body.

He looked at the flushed face, so youthful in its innocent prettiness. He noted the bright eyes, the tremulous mouth, the swift rise and fall of the tilting breasts. He felt an unexpected surge of tenderness that mingled with the racing fever in his blood.

Wanting her, knowing that she was very near to impulsive and generous surrender, he realized that he must be careful not to rush his fences. He must not frighten this innocent and inexperienced girl with the intensity of his ardour. One wrong word, one wrong move, and he might lose her. He held her by a very delicate thread.

There would be plenty of opportunity for teaching her all the delights of sex when they were married. It must be very soon, he decided. For his need was urgent in more ways than one!

He suddenly felt that it was important to set some seal on the agreement. He slipped off the signet ring that he always wore and reached for her left hand. Sliding the heavy ring over her knuckle, he said lightly: "That must do until I can give you a proper engagement ring."

Sylvie was startled. Unsure. She made a last-minute snatch at the remnants of her pride. "I haven't said that I'll marry you!"

Edward kissed her, very lightly. "You said it without words, you know . . ."

And Sylvie supposed that she had.

Later, when he left her, she marvelled at how easily she had slipped into being engaged to Edward Carluke. She had not meant it to happen.

She found it hard to believe that it had happened at all. They had known each other such a short time and surely strangers did not rush into an engagement in this way. But he did not seem like a stranger, she thought, still glowing from his embrace, his kiss. Something within her undoubtedly lifted in swift and instinctive response to him and would not be denied.

But what had happened to her pride, that fierce belief that she could never agree to marry a man who sought only a well-dowered bride and said not a word about loving?

Sylvie did not know. She only knew that she wanted Edward in a way that ought to fill her with shame but only suffused her with eager delight and an ardent anticipation. His kiss, his embrace, held all the promise of an ecstasy that she wanted very much to know.

If marriage was the only key to the world of wonder that she could find in his arms, then she would marry him — and being young and filled with optimism, it did not seem impossible that he might eventually come to love her as she was beginning to love him!

Touched by a strange, new magic, Sylvie found that she could make allowances for his cold-blooded motive for marrying her. She had fallen in love with Chase Hall at first sight. How much dearer it must be to the man who had been born and brought up to its lovely heritage! No wonder he thought it worth any amount of sacrifice . . . even to the extent of marrying a girl he did not and might never love!

She could understand the desire to keep his home and his land at all costs — and he was certainly not the first man to make a marriage of convenience. It had happened many times. Sometimes it was the need for money. Sometimes it was the need for an heir. In Edward's case, it was both — and Sylvie meant to be thankful that he had chosen her rather than the seemingly more suitable Diantha.

Taking heart from his unexpected preference, she told herself that he could not love Diantha . . . and therefore might even learn to love her a little in time.

She was very conscious of the heavy signet ring on her slight hand. It was the Carluke family ring, she knew . . . very old, very valuable. It seemed much more solemn and binding evidence of his intent to marry her than any conventional diamond.

She thought of his arms about her, the warm and kindly reassurance in his dark eyes, and she gradually ceased to tremble, to doubt. It might be madness but she was prepared to trust him even if the world did declare that he was not a man that any woman should trust with her happiness or her peace of mind let alone her heart!

Perhaps the world did not really know him very well, she thought with age-old optimism. Perhaps he had sown all his wild oats and was ready to settle down and really felt that he could be happy with a girl like herself. Perhaps it was not only because she was Hugh Waring's daughter . . .

# 9

SYLVIE was usually down to breakfast before anyone else. But because it was dawn before she finally drifted into a restless and dream-filled sleep, it was late when she descended the stairs the following morning.

Faint shadows beneath the grey eyes and a degree of solemnity in the small face caused Edward to raise an eyebrow as he glanced up from the perusal of the morning papers.

Thankful to find him alone, Sylvie slipped into her usual place at the table beside him, feeling just a little shy. In the cold light of day, it seemed even more unlikely that he could wish to marry her. But the heavy ring on her hand was proof that she had not dreamed his visit to her room and his insistence that he meant to make her his wife.

"That's a gloomy face for a lovely morning," Edward reproached lightly. "Who would believe that you are about to marry the most eligible bachelor in the country bar none, the handsome scion of the noble family of Carluke?"

She did not smile. She looked at him, very grave. "I don't believe it myself."

She looked like a bewildered little girl, so young and innocent, so freshly pretty with her shining hair and serious eyes and sun-kissed skin. She was so sweet, so appealing, so entirely feminine and he liked her more than any girl he had ever known. His instinct told him that such liking could be the prelude to loving.

He had gone to bed with a light heart and slept well and woken to a conviction of coming delight even before he remembered. Now he brushed a strand of hair from her face and kissed her soft cheek. "You may believe it," he said. He reached for her left hand

and touched his ring, smiling into her eyes. "A token of good intent . . . and I intend you nothing but good, my sweet."

The words were light but meaningful. Sylvie's heart swelled at the kiss, the smile, the reassurance and the promise in his dark eyes. She wanted to kiss him, to stroke his dark hair, to put her arms about him like a lover for he was becoming increasingly dear. But she knew she must not overwhelm him with the intensity of her feeling for him. Edward did not care for her and he could not wish her to care for him, she thought, a trifle sadly.

"Are you *sure*?" she asked slowly. "Will you be happy?" She put the question while her heart contracted with the fear that he might seize the opportunity to retract. After all, why should he want her when there were many more suitable brides for a Carluke with just as much to offer as Hugh Waring's daughter? With financial worries weighing on his mind, he might have been prompted by a sudden and swiftly regretted impulse.

Edward was touched by the concern in her quiet voice. She was so sweet, so generous — and really much too good for him, he thought wryly, knowing he must do all in his power to make her happy if they did marry. For all his air of confidence, he was not at all sure that he could keep her on the doubtful path to the altar . . . another reason for ensuring that the marriage took place very soon!

"I hope you haven't been losing sleep over me." He touched the shadows beneath her eyes with very gentle fingers. "*I'm* not sweet and twenty, Sylvie. I know very well what I'm about — *and* what I want." He reached for the coffee-pot, refilled his cup. "You're much too modest," he went on gently, having observed a very natural flicker of doubt in the grey eyes. "I won't pretend to be indifferent to your father's financial circumstances — and I daresay you know that mine are in dire straits! But I should want to marry you even if you weren't Hugh Waring's daughter."

She did not believe him. But it was nice of him to offer that small sop to her pride. "You can't afford to marry where there isn't money, I know," she said with her usual candour. "But as I can't be the only girl in the world with a rich father, I have to believe that you like me a little for myself."

"I like you a lot for yourself," he returned swiftly, warmly. "You're a very sweet girl!"

*Sweet.* Sylvie's heart sank at the dismissive, rather indulgent description. She did not wish to be *sweet* with all its implications of youthful innocence and dull naîvety. She wanted him to think of her as enchanting and exciting and sexy . . . like the beautiful and sophisticated Diantha who seemed to delight him in so many ways. He would tire much too quickly of a sweet young bride, she thought unhappily . . . and she did not think she could bear it if he sought his sexual satisfaction in the arms of other women. She did not want a merely dutiful husband!

Remembering how he had held and kissed her, Sylvie decided that there had been very little ardour in that embrace. It was easy to talk of wanting. There had been very little wanting in the cool, undemanding lips and the lean body against her own, she thought bleakly, unaware of the self-imposed restraint. She had been on fire for him. He had not even tried to take advantage of her obvious weakness where he was concerned!

Edward wondered why his words did not seem to please her. He bent his head to look into her eyes. "Still not sure? It worries me that you've probably lain awake dwelling on my faults," he said lightly.

"It worries me that I know so little about them — or you!" she returned swiftly, frankly.

He chuckled. "Don't worry your pretty head too much about it. My faults are much the same as any other man's, I daresay. Just concentrate on my good points."

"Well, I would . . . if I could think of any," she said sweetly, quite unable to resist.

Their eyes met and exchanged laughing glances. It was one of those moments when Sylvie liked him very, very much — and knew that he liked her. It was a very distinct recommendation for the future and it suddenly dispelled her doubts. For she agreed with him that while the heady excitement of loving probably swept most couples into marriage, it was liking that carried them through the years. If they did not genuinely like each other, then they did not last the course.

"I can supply you with some excellent references," he murmured, eyes dancing.

"From ex-lovers? But who can recommend you as a husband?" she demanded, smiling.

"I'm afraid you must take me on

trust if you mean to take me at all."
He smiled. "Do you, Sylvie?"

"I'm not sure." She had to be
cautious. But in her heart, she knew
that she wanted very much to marry
him.

"Then it's just as well that I haven't
yet dashed off a note to the *Times*
— or informed my Mama," he said
lightly.

Sylvie was silent, twisting his signet
ring round and round on her finger.
Edward studied her, half expecting that
at any moment she would slide it off
and hand it back to him. He knew
apprehension, the stirring of dismay.

Sylvie was hesitating to turn a
beautiful dream into doubtful reality
with a public announcement of their
engagement. Edward might change
his mind. Or, much more likely,
the beautiful Diantha might know
just how to change it for him, she
thought with swift and jealous dislike
of their intimacy.

And, because of that relationship

between Edward and the novelist, the whole world would know that he married her only for the sake of convenience, Sylvie thought with a catch at her heart.

She wanted to marry him so much. But she wished she could feel that she was chosen for her lovable qualities rather than because she was Hugh Waring's daughter.

"Must we tell anyone . . . just yet?"

"Not if you don't wish it." Edward was reassuring. But he was dismayed . . . and a little puzzled. Did she wish for time to talk to Leo, to break the news to him in private? Was she hoping that his friend would insist that such a marriage must not take place, that she must marry him instead?

He felt that Leo was a very real threat. He had swept Sylvie into an engagement with the sheer force of his personality and his will. Leo might yet take possession of her heart by virtue of his much nicer nature and genuinely good qualities.

He could lose Sylvie to a man who spoke of loving and caring for the rest of his life . . . and meant it. Edward was not yet ready to commit himself along those lines . . . and he had already found that it was impossible to lie to the girl whose grey eyes seemed to look deep into his very soul.

Sylvie felt that some explanation was needed. "It's just . . . well, Diantha doesn't like me," she said carefully. "And our engagement puts her in a very humiliating position, Edward. She's leaving in a few days, isn't she? It would be kind to say nothing while she is here as your guest, don't you think?"

It was like her to consider another woman's feelings, Edward thought with swift appreciation of her warmhearted generosity. Any other girl might have been tempted to crow, to flaunt the feather in her cap!

With a tiny prick of conscience, he knew that he had given little thought to Diantha. He did not think that she was much in love with him these days but their relationship had been intimate and he suspected that she had hoped to marry him. It would be a blow to her pride to learn that she had lost him — and to an inexperienced girl!

"Unless Diantha knows, she will continue to expect the lion's share of my attention while she is still here," he pointed out reasonably. "Won't you dislike that?"

"I hope that you won't give me too much cause to dislike it," she said gently.

He laughed. "Clipping my wings already!"

Sylvie hesitated. Then she said carefully: "You will . . . stop seeing Diantha, won't you?"

He smiled at her with understanding. "Yes, of course." He paused. "I can't expect you to approve of the way I've lived my life to date. You know very little of my world. But you may believe that I didn't seduce Diantha with false promises. She went into our affair with eyes wide open and she will accept that it's over without protest, no matter what she feels."

Sylvie looked at him thoughtfully and recalled that he had said nothing to her about loving or loyalty. He was not seducing her with false promises, either. He seemed to be a man of integrity for all the wildness that had earned him his reputation. She was inclined to trust him . . . and perhaps that was more important than loving him, after all.

Late as always, Diantha swept into the room with a blithe greeting, looking very elegant in the colourful and fashionable kaftan, its vivid colours enhancing the glorious hair and the magnolia perfection of her complexion.

She was much too beautiful, Sylvie thought — and wondered if Edward would keep that easily-given promise to end the relationship. She did not feel that she could blame him if he did not!

Diantha smiled at the girl, dropped

a light kiss on Edward's dark hair and turned away to help herself to bacon and kidneys from the covered dishes that were keeping hot on the sideboard.

As she joined them at the table, she fancied a slight constraint in the atmosphere and wondered with amusement if Edward had been making light love to the girl. He was a devil, she thought indulgently. He could not resist the least opportunity for a little meaningless flirtation.

Unused to men like Edward, the girl obviously did not know how to cope with it. At the same time, for all her shy innocence and inexperience, she did not seem tempted to take him at all seriously. Most women responded readily to his charm, his physical magnetism. It seemed to Diantha that Sylvie Waring responded much more readily to Leo's quiet and unassuming and very endearing personality. Diantha was oddly troubled by the steady growth of affection and understanding between them. Surely she had known Leo too long and too well to think of loving him at this late date? Surely she had not loved him all this time without knowing it?

She began to talk to Edward about the day's proposed expedition to the coast with a picnic. Very shortly, Sylvie pushed away her virtually untouched plate and rose to leave them together.

Diantha looked after the girl. "Up to your usual tricks, Edward?" she asked lightly.

He smiled. "You have a very suspicious nature."

She shook her head at him in amused reproach. "She's just a child! She needs protecting from someone like you."

He was suddenly very sober. "Innocence is its own protection, Diantha."

She eyed him sceptically. "I should like to believe that it could keep you at bay!"

He laughed, a little wryly. "It's nice to know that you think so highly of me!"

"Darling, I love you dearly," she told him, smiling. "But I've no illusions about you by this time."

Edward leaned to kiss her lightly on the lips. "I love you, too," he said warmly, liking her very well and just a little sorry that he must allow her to slip out of his life. They had been friends as well as lovers. "We've had some good times . . . "

Diantha raised an eyebrow, a little amused. "Ominous use of past tense. Parting of the ways, Edward?"

She was too shrewd, too perceptive . . . and there was no need to beat about the bush, he decided. She was entitled to the truth. "Sylvie has promised to marry me."

Diantha was flooded with immediate and delighted relief. She had not known until that moment how much it mattered that the girl should not marry Leo! Whether or not she really cared for Edward mattered not at all. Perhaps she had merely played her cards very cleverly. As for Leo's obvious *penchant* for Sylvie, Diantha did not doubt that she could dispel the sentiment if she put her mind to it — and she intended to do just that at the earliest opportunity!

"I'm very pleased," she said, meaning it. "She's a nice child, Edward — better than you deserve and just the kind of wife that a man like you should have! I daresay it will be a very successful marriage."

He was surprised by her reaction. "I didn't expect you to take it so well. I have rather sprung it on you!"

She smiled, a little wryly. "Yes, you have. I thought you were planning to ask me and I've been rehearsing my refusal." He looked at her quickly, a slightly sceptical glow in his dark eyes. "Oh, I know you find that hard to believe," she said, gently mocking. "But we are too much alike, Edward. We'd be leading separate lives within six months! Whereas Sylvie is young enough to expect a great deal from you — and you may find it difficult to disappoint her," she added shrewdly. "By the way, I hope you've told her that you aren't the least bit in love with me!"

"You will appreciate that there is a little awkwardness in mentioning our relationship to the girl I hope to marry," he said dryly.

"But, my dear Edward, there isn't any relationship," she said warmly. "As of now!"

He laughed, understanding. "Just good friends," he suggested lightly.

"Well, I hope so, certainly." She pressed his hand and smiled at him with affection . . .

Leaving her some minutes later, meaning to go in search of Sylvie, something that glinted on the hall table caught Edward's eye. He paused, frowning.

A ray of bright sun fell across a gold signet ring with its unmistakable seal. His ring. Edward picked it up, turned it over in his strong fingers, dark eyes narrowing in sudden anger and apprehension. What the devil was his ring doing on a table in the hall when it should be where it belonged . . . on Sylvie's left hand!

He mounted the stairs two at a time . . .

Sylvie had turned back to collect her unopened letters from the breakfast-table and reached the open door just in time to hear that warm declaration of love on Diantha's lips. Then Edward had kissed her like a lover and returned the answer of a lover and, stricken, she had not waited to see or hear any more.

Shocked into sudden awareness of just how much she loved the man who tried to persuade her into a mockery of marriage with his empty charm and meaningless lovemaking, she had wrenched his ring from her finger and thrown it down on the table on an angry impulse before she fled to her room, blinded by tears.

She could never, never marry him now!

Loving Diantha as he did, he meant to marry her for financial gain — and she could never know peace of mind or any happiness with a husband who obviously hoped to continue his liaison with another woman! How could she marry him and endure the intimacy of his lovemaking with its cold-blooded purpose when she knew just how little she meant!

"*I love you dearly* . . . " Diantha's words with their implication that she loved enough to suffer his marriage to someone else so that he could keep the home and the land that he loved.

"*I love you, too* . . . " Spoken with such warmth and tenderness and unmistakable meaning that Sylvie's heart had swelled with anguish. Unforgettable words that would pierce her with that pain every time they returned to torment her with their echo!

She could never, never marry him now!

But she would not love anyone else

for as long as she lived. She loved Edward with all her heart and soul and being. She wanted him so much . . . rake, rogue, *devil* that he was with his laughing eyes and enchanting smile and the charm that had whisked her heart into his keeping.

Sylvie had recognized her destiny as soon as she set eyes on the handsome Edward Carluke, tall and dark with that distinctive white blaze in his hair and the strong, sensual good looks with the hint of arrogance. Here was her man, she had known quite instinctively. Here was her happiness, now and forever . . .

But she could never, never marry him now!

She began to pack, taking dresses from the wardrobes, filmy lingerie from the drawers.

Edward walked into the room without warning.

Sylvie looked at him, startled and a little apprehensive, her arms full of clothes. His dark eyes were glittering with an anger that she had not seen in him before. Taut, unsmiling, he displayed the signet ring on the palm of his hand.

"Would you like to explain?" He was too angry to be civil.

Her chin lifted at the curt tone. "Isn't it obvious? I decided that I don't wish to marry you, after all." She bundled the collection of garments unceremoniously into a case. "I should like to go home today. Would you arrange for a car to take me to the station, please?" Her voice shook slightly but she was determined that he should not know that her heart was breaking.

"You are entitled to change your mind," he said harshly. "I am entitled to be told in the proper manner, surely? But I suppose it appealed to a youthful sense of the dramatic to leave my ring where I was sure to see it?"

Sylvie tried to close the lid of the overflowing case. He watched her, frowning, refusing to go to her aid. He would not help her to leave his house unless and until she gave him a satisfactory reason for that sudden change of heart.

Silent, Sylvie struggled with the catches of the case. There was nothing she could say. She could not tell him of the pain that had prompted that impulsive and perhaps foolish gesture. She could not mention that lover-like scene that she had witnessed. She could not confess why she had changed her mind about marrying him for he must not know that she loved him!

"Why, Sylvie?" He was tense but controlled.

She knew that he was angry. Thwarted, she thought miserably. It must have seemed that all his problems were soon to be solved. She had fallen into his hands like a ripe plum! And would have married him with a glad heart if she had not overheard that exchange with all its hurtful implications. It seemed to Sylvie, too hurt to be logical or level-headed, that

Diantha was a willing party to his cold-blooded plan to marry Hugh Waring's daughter!

"It wouldn't work." She opened the case again and removed some of the contents, wishing that he would go away and allow her to pack.

She wanted to leave Chase Hall as soon as she could. She wished that she had never accepted Maude Carluke's invitation. She wished that she had never met Edward, never known the swift soaring of her heart at his smile — and never known this bleak despair because he would never love her as she longed to be loved.

Edward was desperate to understand so that he might know the right words to keep her. She had every right to change her mind, of course. She was very young and perhaps she hankered for a more romantic courtship. Maybe he just did not match up to her ideal of all that a lover should be, he thought wryly and with rare humility. He had rushed her into an engagement.

Perhaps he ought to have waited until Diantha had left the Hall and then set himself to convince Sylvie that he was capable of making her happy.

"I thought you were prepared to try," he said carefully without condemnation.

"We don't know each other well enough. It would be a mistake." Trying to be unemotional, her tone came over cold, unfriendly.

He smiled down at her. "We don't have to be married right away . . . "

"No, Edward!" Her control almost snapped at the persuasive warmth in his voice.

A nerve jumped in his jaw. "I need you, Sylvie," he said quietly. He was shaken to realize just how much he needed her. It terrified him that she might walk out of his life for ever.

He had supposed that a man had control over his destiny. He had believed that he could give or keep his heart as he chose. It was a shock to learn that he had lost it without even knowing it!

*Sweet. Enchantingly pretty. A delight and a temptation. A nice girl . . .* He had almost dismissed her with such terms, liking her without suspecting that he loved. Only now did he realize how dear to his heart, how necessary to his happiness, was this girl with her pale hair and honest eyes and appealing innocence.

He loved her deeply. He needed her very much — and for the first time in his life Edward Carluke admitted to a lasting need for someone.

Light-hearted lover that he had been in the past, he had known just how to convince a woman of the strength of his feeling . . . while it lasted. Now, with so much at stake, he did not know the right words, the right moves. He was deterred by the coldness of her attitude, the unmistakable lack of love on her part. He ought to be able to take her into his arms and kiss her into warm response and tell her that he loved her, coax her into loving him. But he could not.

Humbled by a very real love, he doubted that she could love him . . . and he was desperately afraid of losing her completely.

Sylvie's heart contracted. Yes, he needed her, she thought bleakly. Her father's money would be his salvation. He would sacrifice his freedom, his pride, even his happiness with the woman he loved at the altar of his heritage.

"I'm sorry." Her tone was flat, final.

She closed the suitcase and snapped the catches, her back turned to him. Her heart was so full that she was forcing back tears and did not trust herself to look at him.

Edward was only aware of the finality that implied indifference. Loving had not come easily to him. Rejection hit him very hard.

He walked out of the room without another word . . .

# 10

AS the door closed, Sylvie abandoned her packing. She sat down on the bed, her heart thudding with dismay.

Was she about to throw away her only hope of happiness, however slight? Didn't she love Edward? As his wife, she would have every opportunity to weaken and perhaps even break Diantha's hold on him . . . and in time he might even come to love her a little. She was a defeatist!

Pride had compelled her to break their unofficial engagement before it became common knowledge. But there was cold comfort in pride, she thought sadly, appalled by the thought of all the years she must live without the man she loved.

She knew that she would always love him. She could have married him and surely found some joy in just being his wife. Not every marriage began with mutual love, after all.

She was a fool . . . to have had happiness within her grasp and to throw it away! What did it matter that Edward did not love her? He was kind, considerate, even tender. He had said himself that lovers only hurt and disappointed each other because loving asked too much. Perhaps he was very much wiser than herself. He seemed very sure that they could build a successful marriage . . . and he had promised to end his affair with Diantha. Why did she doubt him so much?

She was roused by a little commotion in the corridor outside her room, raised voices. She went to the door, curious and slightly alarmed.

Lady Carluke's maid seemed to be involved in some kind of altercation with a stern-faced Edward. As she opened the door, they both turned towards her — and Mary seemed thankful to see her while Edward's frown deepened.

"Is anything wrong?" she asked involuntarily.

"Oh, miss . . . could you come to my lady?" It was an unmistakable appeal.

Sylvie felt a little catch of apprehension at her heart. She looked instinctively to Edward. "What is it?"

"Apparently my mother is not very well this morning — and I am at a loss to know why I was not informed much earlier!" he said harshly.

The maid turned to him, obviously on the defensive. "My lady wouldn't have you worried, sir — and you know that she can be very stubborn. It doesn't do to argue with her when she's getting over an attack. She didn't seem too badly at first but now . . . well, I'm worried about her, I will admit. But she won't take her pills or settle until she's seen Miss Waring."

"I'll come, of course. Have you sent for Dr Lovell?"

"Yes, miss. He was out on a call but

his wife said she would contact him and send him along directly."

Sylvie nodded. "I'll see if I can persuade her to take her pills in the meantime." She touched the woman's arm and smiled reassuringly. She knew that Mary had been with Lady Carluke for many years and was deeply attached to her mistress. "I'm sure she will be fine. Don't worry."

"Oh, I do hope so, miss!" She blinked back tears.

Edward walked along the corridor with Sylvie. Glancing at his set face, she felt for his natural anxiety, knowing that he was a very devoted son.

She said gently: "I expect Mary is alarming us unnecessarily. Your mother recovers from these attacks very quickly as a rule, doesn't she?"

"She has been having them for some years. I'm afraid we have all fallen into the trap of treating them much too lightly," he said wryly. He looked down at her, hesitating. Then he added, somewhat brusquely: "Mary was insisting that my mother wished for you and I was trying to keep her from disturbing you. It seemed the wrong moment to be involving you in my family concerns."

Sylvie thought that he must feel it very much that his mother wished for a newcomer instead of himself. "But I am family, Edward," she said quietly.

"Yes, of course," he remembered. He smiled, rueful. "I haven't been thinking of you as a cousin, I must admit. But my Mama seems to look upon you as the daughter she would have liked. She is very fond of you, Sylvie."

A little colour stole into her face and her heart wrenched anew at the reminder of the marriage that might have been. She wondered if he meant to make her feel guilty. After all, she had let him down and it would be very natural if he were resentful.

"She has been very kind to me," she said, a little stiffly. They reached the door of his mother's room. "Give me a moment to persuade her to take her pills and then I'll call you in to see for yourself that she's all right."

He nodded. "Very well . . . "

Sylvie longed to take his dear face between her hands and kiss the apprehension from the dark eyes. She contented herself with finding his hand and pressing it briefly, reassuringly.

As she entered the room, she braced herself for the possibility that death was hovering. The maid's obvious anxiety and apprehension had communicated itself quite forcibly.

Maude turned her head. Her fingers were fretting at the coverlet and her eyes were anxious but determined. She was a poor colour and there was a hint of mauve about her lips and her breathing was shallow and slightly distressed. "My dear . . . " She held out a thin hand, almost supplicating.

Sylvie took it in both her own, smiled down at her elderly cousin with warm affection, tried to hide her swift anxiety. "What is all this nonsense about not

234

taking your pills?" she scolded gently, like a loving daughter.

Maude smiled weakly. "I'm not in any pain, child." It was an obvious effort for her to talk and her voice was thready. "Mary thinks I ought to sleep and I will — but I must talk to you first."

"I don't think you should tire yourself with talking . . . "

"I don't feel that I have very much time," Maude returned without emotion. "It may be now or never, my dear."

Sylvie did not mean to agitate her with argument. She was obviously very ill. "Very well . . . but take your pills first," she said firmly, reaching for the small bottle and the glass of water.

Maude swallowed them without further protest. Then she drew Sylvie down to sit on the side of the bed. "You're such a good girl . . . a very dear girl," she said warmly. "So like your mother . . . " She patted Sylvie's hand. "I was so fond of your dear mother, you know."

"I really think you should rest now," Sylvie said gently. "You'll feel so much better when you've slept for a few hours. I know that you've had a bad night. Do let me call Edward in for a few words with you and then try to sleep . . ."

"Edward." Maude's tone softened. "Dear Edward . . . that's what I wanted to speak to you about, child. You love him, don't you?" She smiled with affectionate understanding and touched her hand to the soft cheek that was suddenly suffused with colour. "I know you do . . . just as I loved his father," she went on tenderly. "And Edward is a much better man, you know. He won't break your heart . . . and it is quite true that reformed rakes make the best husbands, my dear. Promise me that you'll marry my son . . ." The long speech had tired her and she lay back against the pillows, very pale, very frail.

Sylvie did not know what to say. She

was terribly afraid that Lady Carluke might be dying and she ought not to be distressed by a blunt refusal of her request. But if she made such a promise at such a time and then failed to keep it, how could she live with her conscience?

She decided on a compromise. She lifted one of the fine, thin hands to her lips and kissed it, feeling affection and concern for her cousin. "I do love Edward," she said quietly, voicing it aloud for the very first time. "But I can't make that promise, I'm afraid. I don't believe that he would be happy if he married me."

"He certainly won't be happy with that woman!" The shallow breath quickened and Sylvie felt the fluttering of the pulse in the thin wrist. Her own heart leaped with concern. "Oh, my dear . . . if he asks you to marry him you must say yes! Promise me!"

Sylvie thought it best not to admit that Edward had asked and been rejected. "Yes, I will," she soothed, very sure that he was much too proud to risk a second rebuff. "If Edward asks me . . ."

The door opened. "Lovell is here at last," Edward announced with evident relief. He moved to the bed. "Mama, how are you feeling? What do you mean by having us all by the ears when you are obviously as right as rain!" He bent down to kiss her brow, a very tender light in his dark eyes. She clung to him. "Have you taken your pills?"

"Dear Edward . . ."

"Dear Mama . . ." He smiled down at her, very loving.

Sylvie slipped from the room as the doctor entered with Mary at his heels, desperately hoping that Edward's keen ears had not made sense of that urgent conversation behind the closed door. She had admitted to loving him . . . but she could never admit it to Edward himself!

Choked with emotion, she made her way back to her room. There, she began to unpack and put away her clothes. Obviously she could not leave the Hall that day as she had intended.

Her cousin might need her . . . and if she died, then Edward might need her, she thought with a little hope in her heart. She was family, after all, however remote the connection. It might comfort him to talk to her, to know that she also grieved. His mother had treated her like a dear daughter in the few weeks that they had known each other.

Anxious for some news, she went down to wait in the hall. When the doctor left, she would probably have a chance to speak to him or Edward.

Hero rose from her usual corner and padded across the parquet floor to nuzzle Sylvie's hand with a little whimper, obviously sensitive to the anxiety and unease in the house. She made a fuss of the elderly dog . . . and glanced up as a tall shadow fell across the sunlit hall. Leo hesitated on the threshold, smiling at her.

She straightened and went to greet him.

"Diantha telephoned," he said, concerned. "How is Lady Carluke?"

"Not very well, I'm afraid. The doctor is with her now."

"I thought there might be something I could do . . . ?"

She smiled at him gratefully. "I don't think so. But it's lovely to see you, of course. I'm sure Diantha will be pleased that you've come over. We are all rather upset and I imagine she is being neglected." She looked about her absently. "I'm not sure where she is at the moment . . . "

"Would you like me to take her off your hands?" he asked gently, with sympathy.

If only you would — for ever! It was an instinctive and very heartfelt reaction that she did not dare to put into words.

"I think Edward would be grateful if you were kind enough to look after her for a few hours, certainly," she said carefully.

"It isn't kindness on my part," he said, with a little smile in the very blue eyes. "It's entirely selfish. I think you know that I would gladly look after Diantha for the rest of her life . . . if she would only give me the chance!"

Sylvie looked at him affectionately. "Yes, I do know," she said gently.

"So do I . . . *now*!" Diantha said dryly from the door of the drawing-room. "But I do think you might have told me first, Leo."

He spun on his heel at the sound of her drawling voice, startled and a little dismayed. Then, as he saw the encouraging smile in her beautiful eyes, he looked at her with his heart in his own. "Diantha . . . "

Her smile was suddenly tremulous and there was a most unusual quiver in that cool voice as she said lightly: "I don't know why you didn't look at me like that before, darling idiot! A woman does some stupid things when she

241

thinks she isn't loved, you know . . . "

He moved towards her with newfound confidence and unmistakable intent . . . and Sylvie melted tactfully into the background, knowing herself forgotten.

She went into the library and closed the door, her own emotions in a very muddled state. She ought to be sorry that Edward had lost the woman he loved to his friend. She was deeply thankful that Diantha had reacted so surprisingly to Leo's quiet and heartfelt words.

She was far from believing that Edward would look to her for consolation . . . and she did not know that she wanted to be a substitute for the woman who had disappointed and deserted him.

She could not help feeling that if she were to marry Edward, they would have a better chance of success with Diantha safely and happily married to someone else. But how could she marry him now? How could she go to him and admit that she had changed her mind again and would like very much to be his wife, after all . . . ?"

Edward opened the door and glanced into the room. "Sylvie . . . ?"

She rose from her chair. "Yes, I'm here . . . " She went to him and searched the dark eyes with some anxiety in her own.

He gave her a small, reassuring smile. "It's all right. She's sleeping."

Sylvie released her pent breath. "Really all right?"

"Lovell won't commit himself. He says she will need careful nursing for a few days." He sat down heavily, running a hand through his hair.

She put a hand on his shoulder, tentatively. "I shall be glad to do anything I can," she said warmly.

He did not look at her. "Lovell is bringing in a couple of nurses to take care of her . . . and some special equipment, apparently."

Sylvie felt snubbed. "I see. Then you won't need me," she said brightly, hiding her hurt.

"In the circumstances, you wish to leave the Hall, of course," he said quietly. "Obviously, I appreciate your feelings. But I'd be very grateful if you would agree to stay for a few more days. I think my mother will be happier to know that you are near. She has come to depend on you quite a lot, apparently . . ."

"Please don't mind, Edward," she said warmly, feeling swift compassion for him. "It's only that women always turn to their own sex when they are ill. She needs you much more, really. She loves you so much!"

Edward looked up at her, smiling, moved by the impulsive words that betrayed a warm concern for his supposed sensitivity. She was so sweet, so very dear.

"Yes, I know. And I don't mind at all. You must forgive me if I have given the impression that I do. I'm not jealous of my Mama's affection for you, Sylvie. You have supplied a need that I didn't even know to exist." For me as much as my Mama, he thought on a surge of loving tenderness and longing.

She regarded him like a solemn, tender-hearted child, grey eyes wide with anxious concern. She had so much capacity for caring. If only she cared for him, he thought with an ache that was becoming almost unbearable.

He leaned back against the sofa cushions, closing his eyes. Suddenly he felt very, very weary. And despondent. He had lived for years with the knowledge of his mother's heart condition and, as he had said to Sylvie, he had become inured by the frequent but not serious attacks into supposing that she would live for many years to come. He loved her dearly and he had been shocked by the day's events into realizing that his beautiful home would be a very bleak and lonely place without her gracious and loving presence.

More than ever, he needed a wife, friend and companion and lover. More than ever, he needed Sylvie for it was impossible to contemplate marrying anyone else. If he could not have her then he would not marry at all, he knew. For what was the Hall and its cherished acres to him if he could not share it with the woman he loved?

Sylvie had slipped so naturally into the rôle of surrogate daughter to his mother . . . and she seemed to have had a place in his heart and in his life since the very beginning of time. He could not now visualize any other woman as his love, his wife, the mother of his children and the mistress of his home.

He had not known that loving could fill a man's heart and mind to the exclusion of almost every other consideration. He had not known that it was possible to be so utterly in thrall to a sweet face, a shy smile, a gentle voice and manner.

Sylvie was so lovely — and he loved her. Sylvie was warm and kind and thoughtful — and he loved her. Sylvie had a loving heart and that counted for more than anything else in a woman — and he loved her. He wished with all his heart that she loved him . . .

Studying him, Sylvie ached for his obvious unhappiness, the anxiety he must feel. She yearned to put her arms about him and hold him, wished she could believe that it would comfort him at all to know that she cared.

Instead, she crossed the room to the decanters and poured whisky into a glass for him, feeling that he was probably in need of a drink at this particular time. It was little enough to do for him, she thought wistfully, wishing she could do so much more.

Edward stirred at her light touch on his shoulder, the quiet utterance of his name. She offered the glass, smiling with that endearing hint of shyness in the grey eyes. He resisted the irresistible temptation to draw her close and forget his pain in the sweet warmth of her lips. He must not force himself on a girl who did not want him, he thought humbly. He had to accept that he had no place in her heart, in her future, no matter how dear she was to him or how bleak his future seemed without the hope of sharing it with her.

He smiled his thanks as he took the glass from her hand. It was not surprising that his mother was so fond of this gentle, thoughtful girl. She endeared herself in so many ways.

The whisky seared his throat. He gave a little gasp. "What happened to the soda?"

"Did I make it too strong? I thought you might be glad of a stiff drink. This is a very difficult time for you," she said quietly.

"In more ways than one," he agreed, grim, not meaning to reproach her but unable to keep just a hint of bitterness from the words. He was struggling with a wave of despair and the conviction that he was entirely unlovable in the eyes of this dear girl.

Sylvie thought he referred to Diantha's sudden and astonishing preference for

Leo. She looked at him, very grave. "I'm so sorry, Edward." Her tone was very gentle.

He rose abruptly, moved to add a dash of soda water to his whisky. "Do you mind if we don't talk about it?" He drained the glass and set it down with a little snap.

Sylvie made instant allowances for the harsh tone. Poor Edward! Everything was suddenly going wrong for him, she thought with warm compassion. She had refused to solve his financial difficulties by marrying him. Now Diantha had transferred her affections to Leo without warning. It must seem to him that he had no hope of settling his debts in the near future and keeping his beloved Hall and its glorious acres. To cap everything else, he had the anxiety of his mother's critical state of health.

She gazed at him with a very full heart, loving him, longing to comfort him . . . and the pride that had tried so hard to fly high seemed to be stifled by the powerful emotion in her breast. She loved him. She wanted him with all her heart. She wanted his peace of mind even if she could not ensure his happiness. Nothing else seemed to matter at that moment.

Impulsively, moved by love, she ran to him and put her arms about him, saying his name on a breathless murmur, kissing him with her heart on her lips.

Taken by surprise, he had sufficient presence of mind to enfold her in his own arms, his heart soaring because of her unsuspected need of him. Her lips were warm and very sweet and just a little shy.

Edward caught his breath. His arms tightened about her with new urgency. "Sylvie . . . oh, Sylvie," he whispered as wave after wave of tender loving swept through him. He held her very close, his heart very thankful that by some miracle it had won its dearest wish. "My dear, dear love," he said softly.

She clung to him, weak with wanting, her heart scarcely daring to believe the promise in the way he held and kissed her, the way he spoke her name. He loved her! Just as she loved him! His touch, his kiss, his embrace and the warm tone all spoke of a loving she had not dared to dream that he might ever know for her. His arms were her safe harbour, his tender kiss the assurance of so much happiness to come.

"Edward . . . " She drew away slightly.

He smiled down at her, very tender. "My darling?"

She trembled at his tone, the look in his dark eyes. She needed no other proof of loving in a man who had been reputed to be without heart. "Your mother wishes me to marry you," she said tremulously.

"My Mama is a very wise woman." He kissed the soft, pale hair that framed her sweet face and traced the curve of her cheek to the corner of her mouth. She turned her head eagerly and with unashamed delight to meet his lips and his heart quickened with love. She was enchanting, a dear delight, his love now and forever!

"I promised that I would . . . " Sylvie was breathless with the excitement that his kiss evoked and stirred by the promise of ecstasy. Her heart fluttered in her breast like a wild bird.

He held her away from him. "You'd marry me to please my mother?" He spoke lightly, gently mocking. He knew very well that his feeling for her had inspired a miraculous response in this dear, lovely girl and he would be eternally thankful. He meant to spend the rest of his life in ensuring her happiness, her contentment.

Sylvie smiled up at him, a golden smile that conveyed all her love, all her longing. "To please myself, Edward," she said softly.

She put her arms about his neck and gave her lips to him in a kiss that was sweet and yielding surrender to her need of him. He cradled her head in a strong hand, his heart welling with the kind of love that he had never felt for any woman until Sylvie came into his life.

"I love you so much," he murmured against her lips. "Please marry me, Sylvie . . ."

She sighed a little sigh of deep content and nestled into the warm sanctuary of his embrace. Life with a man who loved her as much as she loved him would surely be her greatest happiness this side of heaven . . .

## THE END

## WITH SOMEBODY ELSE
### Theresa Charles

Rosamond sets off for Cornwall with Hugo to meet his family, blissfully unaware of the shocks in store for her.


## A SUMMER FOR STRANGERS
### Claire Hamilton

Because she had lost her job, her flat and she had no money, Tabitha agreed to pose as Adam's future wife although she believed the scheme to be deceitful and cruel.


## VILLA OF SINGING WATER
### Angela Petron

The disquieting incidents that occurred at the Vatican and the Colosseum did not trouble Jan at first, but then they became increasingly unpleasant and alarming.

## DOCTOR NAPIER'S NURSE
### Pauline Ash

When cousins Midge and Derry are entered as probationer nurses on the same day but at different hospitals they agree to exchange identities.

## A GIRL LIKE JULIE
### Louise Ellis

Caroline absolutely adored Hugh Barrington, but then Julie Crane came into their lives. Julie was the kind of girl who attracts men without even trying.

## COUNTRY DOCTOR
### Paula Lindsay

When Evan Richmond bought a practice in a remote country village he did not realise that a casual encounter would lead to the loss of his heart.

# ENCORE
## Helga Moray

Craig and Janet realise that their true happiness lies with each other, but it is only under traumatic circumstances that they can be reunited.

# NICOLETTE
## Ivy Preston

When Grant Alston came back into her life, Nicolette was faced with a dilemma. Should she follow the path of duty or the path of love?

# THE GOLDEN PUMA
## Margaret Way

Catherine's time was spent looking after her father's Queensland farm. But what life was there without David, who wasn't interested in her?

## HOSPITAL BY THE LAKE
### Anne Durham

Nurse Marguerite Ingleby was always ready to become personally involved with her patients, to the despair of Brian Field, the Senior Surgical Registrar, who loved her.

## VALLEY OF CONFLICT
### David Farrell

Isolated in a hostel in the French Alps, Ann Russell sees her fiancé being seduced by a young girl. Then comes the avalanche that imperils their lives.

## NURSE'S CHOICE
### Peggy Gaddis

A proposal of marriage from the incredibly handsome and wealthy Reagan was enough to upset any girl — and Brooke Martin was no exception.

## A DANGEROUS MAN
### Anne Goring

Photographer Polly Burton was on safari in Mombasa when she met enigmatic Leon Hammond. But unpredictability was the name of the game where Leon was concerned.

## PRECIOUS INHERITANCE
### Joan Moules

Karen's new life working for an authoress took her from Sussex to a foreign airstrip and a kidnapping; to a real life adventure as gripping as any in the books she typed.

## VISION OF LOVE
### Grace Richmond

When Kathy takes over the rundown country kennels she finds Alec Stinton, a local vet, very helpful. But their friendship arouses bitter jealousy and a tragedy seems inevitable.

## CRUSADING NURSE
### Jane Converse

It was handsome Dr. Corbett who opened Nurse Susan Leighton's eyes and who set her off on a lonely crusade against some powerful enemies and a shattering struggle against the man she loved.

## WILD ENCHANTMENT
### Christina Green

Rowan's agreeable new boss had a dream of creating a famous perfume using her precious Silverstar, but Rowan's plans were very different.

## DESERT ROMANCE
### Irene Ord

Sally agrees to take her sister Pam's place as La Chartreuse the dancer, but she finds out there is more to it than dyeing her hair red and looking like her sister.

## HEART OF ICE
### Marie Sidney

How was January to know that not only would the warmth of the Swiss people thaw out her frozen heart, but that she too would play her part in helping someone to live again?

## LUCKY IN LOVE
### Margaret Wood

Companion-secretary to wealthy gambler Laura Duxford, who lived in Monaco, seemed to Melanie a fabulous job. Especially as Melanie had already lost her heart to Laura's son, Julian.

## NURSE TO PRINCESS JASMINE
### Lilian Woodward

Nick's surgeon brother, Tom, performs an operation on an Arabian princess, and she invites Tom, Nick and his fiancé to Omander, where a web of deceit and intrigue closes about them.

## THE WAYWARD HEART
### Eileen Barry

Disaster-prone Katherine's nickname was "Kate Calamity", but her boss went too far with an outrageous proposal, which because of her latest disaster, she could not refuse.

## FOUR WEEKS IN WINTER
### Jane Donnelly

Tessa wasn't looking forward to meeting Paul Mellor again — she had made a fool of herself over him once before. But was Orme Jared's solution to her problem likely to be the right one?

## SURGERY BY THE SEA
### Sheila Douglas

Medical student Meg hadn't really wanted to go and work with a G.P. on the Welsh coast although the job had its compensations. But Owen Roberts was certainly not one of them!

## HEAVEN IS HIGH
### Anne Hampson

The new heir to the Manor of Marbeck had been found. But it was rather unfortunate that when he arrived unexpectedly he found an uninvited guest, complete with stetson and high boots.

## LOVE WILL COME
### Sarah Devon

June Baker's boss was not really her idea of her ideal man, but when she went from third typist to boss's secretary overnight she began to change her mind.

## ESCAPE TO ROMANCE
### Kay Winchester

Oliver and Jean first met on Swale Island. They were both trying to begin their lives afresh, but neither had bargained for complications from the past.

## CASTLE IN THE SUN
### Cora Mayne

Emma's invalid sister, Kym, needed a warm climate, and Emma jumped at the chance of a job on a Mediterranean island. But Emma soon finds that intrigues and hazards lurk on the sunlit isle.

## BEWARE OF LOVE
### Kay Winchester

Carol Brampton resumes her nursing career when her family is killed in a car accident. With Dr. Patrick Farrell she begins to pick up the pieces of her life, but is bitterly hurt when insinuations are made about her to Patrick.

## DARLING REBEL
### Sarah Devon

When Jason Farradale's secretary met with an accident, her glamorous stand-in was quite unable to deal with one problem in particular.

## THE PRICE OF PARADISE
### Jane Arbor

It was a shock to Fern to meet her estranged husband on an island in the middle of the Indian Ocean, but to discover that her father had engineered it puzzled Fern. What did he hope to achieve?

## DOCTOR IN PLASTER
### Lisa Cooper

When Dr. Scott Sutcliffe is injured, Nurse Caroline Hurst has to cope with a very demanding private case. But when she realises her exasperating patient has stolen her heart, how can Caroline possibly stay?

## A TOUCH OF HONEY
### Lucy Gillen

Before she took the job as secretary to author Robert Dean, Cadie had heard how charming he was, but that wasn't her first impression at all.

## ROMANTIC LEGACY
### Cora Mayne

As kennelmaid to the Armstrongs, Ann Brown, had no idea that she would become the central figure in a web of mystery and intrigue.

## THE RELENTLESS TIDE
### Jill Murray

Steve Palmer shared Nurse Marie Blane's love of the sea and small boats. Marie's other passion was her step-brother. But when danger threatened who should she turn to — her step-brother or the man who stirred emotions in her heart?

## ROMANCE IN NORWAY
### Cora Mayne

Nancy Crawford hopes that her visit to Norway will help her to start life again. She certainly finds many surprises there, including unexpected happiness.